# SHE IS NOT INVISIBLE

*Also by Marcus Sedgwick*

Blood Red, Snow White
The Book of Dead Days
The Dark Flight Down
The Dark Horse
Floodland
The Foreshadowing
The Kiss of Death
Midwinterblood
Revolver
My Swordhand is Singing
White Crow
Witch Hill

*And series for younger readers*

**The Raven Mysteries**

**Elf Girl and Raven Boy**

For more information visit –
www.marcussedgwick.com

# SHE IS NOT INVISIBLE

## MARCUS SEDGWICK

Indigo

First published in Great Britain in 2013
by Indigo
a division of the Orion Publishing Group Ltd
Orion House
5 Upper St Martin's Lane
London WC2H 9EA
A Hachette UK Company

5 7 9 10 8 6 4

A catalogue record for this book is
available from the British Library.

ISBN 978 1 78062 109 8

Printed in Great Britain by
Clays Ltd, St Ives plc

The Orion Publishing Group's policy is to use papers
that are natural, renewable and recyclable products made
from wood grown in sustainable forests. The logging and
manufacturing processes are expected to conform to the
environmental regulations of the country of origin.

www.orionbooks.co.uk

For Alice, just for being cool.

If a man look sharply and attentively, he shall see Fortune: for though she be blind, yet she is not invisible.

Francis Bacon – '*Of Fortune*', 1612

# Contents

The First Gate          13

The Black Book          25

You Never Know          39

The Guard Dogs          51

The First Page          63

The Stray Book          69

The Third Gate          79

The Right Seat          85

The Plane Trip 93

The Fizzy Tist 103

The Blind Hero 109

Who Knows What? 125

The Third Page 133

One Blind Girl 139

One Money Size 149

One Weird Dude 157

Two Crazy Guys 171

The Black King 179

354 193

The Empty Room 203

The Dying Poet 215

The Poet's Home                223

The Pious Poem                 237

And Third Long                 243

The Human Mind                 253

The Fatal Idea                 267

Two Dried Mice                 281

The Final Clue                 291

God Plays Dice                 297

The Wrong Idea                 309

The Noisy City                 319

One Giant Leap                 329

Boy Meets Girl                 335

## *The First Gate*

One final time I told myself I wasn't abducting my little brother.

I swear I hadn't even *thought* of it that way until we were on the Underground, and by the time we got to the airport, it was too late for second thoughts, and it was too late to put Mum's credit card back in her purse.

It was also too late *not* to have used that credit card to buy us, Benjamin and me, two tickets to New York, and it was without a shadow of a doubt far too late *not* to have taken out five hundred dollars from the fancy-pants cashpoint at the airport.

But I *had* done all these things, though I passed at least some of the blame on to Mum for letting me help her with online shopping from time to time, as well as telling me most of her pin numbers.

However many crimes I'd committed already that morning, I'd done it all for a very good reason, and it must be said that they faded into insignificance next to the thought that I was abducting my brother.

Benjamin, to his credit, was taking the whole thing as only a slightly strange seven-year-old can. He stood patiently, holding my hand, his *Watchmen* backpack on his back, silently waiting for me to get myself together. Far from screaming to the world that his big sister was kidnapping him, he was much more concerned with whether Stan needed a ticket.

 I held his hand tightly. We were somewhere in the check-in hall at Terminal 3. It was loud and very confusing and we needed to find the right desk. People hurried by on all sides and I'd already lost track of where we'd come in.

'Stan does not need a ticket,' I repeated, for the eleventy-eighth time, and before Benjamin could get in his bonus question added, 'And no, he does not need a passport either.'

'But we do,' said Benjamin. He sounded a little nervous. If Stan didn't make the flight I knew Benjamin's world would probably end.

'Yes,' I said. 'We do.'

Just then, by coincidence I heard someone walk past talking about a flight to New York, and that started me panicking.

I took a long, slow breath. Benjamin is utterly wonderful and I love him deeply, but he does have his moments, and I needed him. I *absolutely* needed him; if I didn't, I wouldn't have *abducted* him. Not that I had. Not really.

'We do,' I explained, 'because we are real, alive, and human, and Stan, exceptional though he is, is none of those things.'

Benjamin thought about this for a moment.

'He is real,' he said.

'Yes, you're right,' I said. 'Sorry. He is real. But he's also a stuffed toy. He doesn't need a passport.'

'Are you really sure?'

'I'm really sure. How is he, anyway?'

Benjamin held a brief conference with Stan. I

15

guessed he was probably holding him by the wing, as usual, in the same way I was holding Benjamin's hand. We must have looked pretty silly, the three of us. Me, then pint-sized Benjamin, then a scruffy black raven.

'He's fine, but he misses everyone.'

By everyone Benjamin meant the menagerie of fluffy creatures and plastic superheroes in his bedroom.

'We only left them an hour ago.'

'I know, but that's just how Stan is. He also says he's missing Dad.'

I pulled Benjamin into a walk.

'Listen, Benjamin. You need to find the desk that says Virgin Atlantic Check-In. Maybe Stan can help. Don't ravens have excellent eyesight?'

It was a bit of a gamble but it worked.

'Virgin Atlantic . . . ' Benjamin repeated. 'Come on. It's right here! Stan, I beat you. Even though you have excellent eyesight.'

Benjamin started ahead, quickly, and I hung on to him, tugging his hand to try to get him to remember how we walk. It's something we worked out together a couple of years ago and he likes doing

16

it, but I guess he was excited about going on a plane again, and his hand slipped out of mine as he trotted away.

'Benjamin!' I called, waiting for him to come back.

It was probably only a second or two but I freaked out and rushed after him, then kicked into a bag or something, and went sprawling full length on the floor.

Even in the noise of the airport I heard everyone around me go quiet as they watched and I knew I'd made a stunning spectacle of myself. I'd landed with my legs over the bag and my arms flung out in front of me.

'Am I invisible?' a man said, angrily.

My sunglasses had shot off my face somewhere and I heard him sigh.

'Why don't you look where you're going? My laptop's in there.'

I got to my feet and managed to kick his bag again.

'For God's sake,' he said.

'I'm sorry,' I muttered. 'Sorry.'

I kept my head down as the man unzipped his bag, grumbling.

'Benjamin?' I said, but he was already back at my side.

'Are you okay, Laureth?' he asked, pushing something into my hands. 'Here's your glasses.'

I slipped them on quickly.

'I'm really sorry,' I said in the direction of the man, and held my hand out for Benjamin to take. 'We'd better get a move on.'

Benjamin took my hand and this time walked with me properly, in our secret way.

'There's a queue,' he said, coming to a stop. 'It's only short.'

The first gate, I said to myself. That's what Dad would have called it. The first person I had to pass; the assistant at the check-in desk.

'It's our go,' whispered Benjamin.

'Next customer, please!'

It was the woman at the desk.

I squeezed Benjamin's hand, and bent down to whisper back.

'Wait here.'

'Why?'

'You know why,' I said, which gave me the task of walking the few paces up to the desk by myself.

I was glad it was summer, and hot outside, because it looks less weird wearing sunglasses when the sun's shining, even indoors, but after falling over some grumpy guy's bag I didn't want to draw any more attention to myself.

'Where are you travelling today?' asked the woman, before I was even at the desk.

I thought about my friend Harry at school. He's amazing. He'd have tried making a couple of clicks to figure out where the desk was, but I guessed it probably wouldn't have worked even for him; there was way too much background noise. Besides, there's always the risk that someone thinks you're pretending to be a dolphin. Not cool. Instead, I swept my hands up slowly but smoothly, and was very pleased that I'd got the distance almost exactly right. I mean, I banged my shins painfully into some kind of metal foot rail in front of the desk, but I did my best to keep a straight face and plonked our passports on the desk.

'Er, New York,' I said. 'JFK. 9:55.'

The woman took our passports.

'Any bags to check in?'

'Er, no,' I said. 'Just hand baggage.'

I turned and showed her my backpack, and waved a hand towards Benjamin, praying he'd stayed where I'd left him.

'Short break, is it? Doing anything nice?'

I told her the truth. What I hoped was the truth.

'Going to see our dad,' I said.

She paused.

'How old are you, Miss Peak?'

'Sixteen.'

'And that's your brother, is it?'

I nodded.

'And he's . . . ?'

'Oh, he's seven. It said on the website he can travel with me if he's five. And he's seven. And I'm sixteen, so I, I mean we, we thought that . . . '

'Oh yes,' said the woman, 'that's fine, I was just asking. But does the bird have a passport?'

'I told you!' cried Benjamin from somewhere behind me.

'It's okay, love,' said the woman. 'I'm joking. He doesn't need a passport.'

'He doesn't need a passport,' I said. Then I felt stupid and shut up.

'Can I have a look at your bird?' the woman said,

over my shoulder.

'I have to stay here,' said Benjamin.

'Why does he have to stay there?' said the woman to me.

Suddenly things were going in the wrong direction.

'You know,' I said, trying a smile. 'Small boys. I mean, he doesn't have to stay there, but well, small boys.'

'Are you okay, Miss Peak?' the woman asked. Her voice was suddenly serious.

'Oh. Yes. You know. Anxious.'

'The flight's not for an hour and a half. You've plenty of time.'

'Oh, no,' I said, feeling more desperate to get away than ever. 'I mean about flying. And you know, there's Benjamin.'

I heard her laugh.

'Twins,' she announced. 'My boys are such a handful, and just his age. And there's two of them, so count yourself lucky. Whenever we go on holiday it's like we've declared war on the poor country.'

I laughed. I thought I sounded really nervous, but the woman didn't seem to notice.

'Have a nice flight,' she said.

She put the passports back on the desk.

'Boarding is 8:55. Should be gate 35. For your own reassurance it would be sensible to watch for any changes.'

So then there was just the small issue of picking the passports back up off the counter. I made a gentle sweep across the desk and with relief found them straight away.

'Thank you,' I said. 'Benjamin. Hold my hand. You know how you get lost so easily.'

Benjamin came over and took my hand.

'I don't!' he protested, and then, since he was being indignant about it, forgot to squeeze my hand to show me which way to go.

I froze, though what I really wanted to do was get him away from the nice woman's desk before he could do any serious damage.

'Which way do we go?' I asked her.

'Departures is upstairs,' she said. 'Escalators are over there.'

'Benjamin,' I said. 'Benjamin? Shall we . . . ?'

But, bless him, by then he was already pulling me away from the desk, in the right direction. He's remarkably good to me, mostly.

The first gate had been passed.

'Are we going to find Daddy now?' Benjamin asked, as we rode up the escalators to Departures.

'Yes,' I said. 'We're going to find Daddy now.'

# *The Black Book*

Thing: a word which Mr Woodell, my English teacher, tells me I use way too much. But sometimes there is no better word to use than *thing*.

For example, there are a couple of vital things to know when abducting your little brother, even if you're not really: thing one, it's much simpler if he doesn't know you're abducting him, and thing two, it makes the guilt easier to bear if you have a really good reason *why* you're abducting him.

I passed both of these with flying colours.

On thing one, Benjamin was perfect. Old enough

to be useful, young enough not to know that you don't just leave your house early on a Saturday morning to fly to America with your big sister.

'Isn't Mummy coming?' he'd asked, when I'd woken him.

'Mummy's going to Auntie Sarah's today, don't you remember?'

It was only seven o'clock, and on a Saturday morning at that. Mum had already left, to beat the worst of the traffic to Manchester, she said, leaving me with strict instructions about when to get Benjamin up, what to get him to eat and so on, as if I didn't do it a lot anyway. When I'm home at weekends and in the holidays I often look after Benjamin because Mum's shifts can be dead awkward. So she's not there a lot and Dad, well, Dad's often away these days. With the fairies, Mum says.

mmq

As for thing two; that had only begun the evening before, when I'd checked Dad's email for him. Dad pays me twenty pounds a month to check his fan mail and other random communications that come via his website. I'd started doing it for him when he was

26

away on trips, but pretty soon he asked me to check it all the time, since I was doing it so well and since it made him less stressed not to have to read every single one.

I tell Dad if there's anything important that he needs to know, and otherwise I send back one of the standard replies that he has saved in a folder on the desktop, always at hand, because ninety per cent of the emails fall into one of three categories.

There's the reply for 'I am an aspiring writer and I would like you to read what I've written.' There's the reply for 'I read your book and I loved it, please will you write more.' And there's the reply for 'I have a question for you; where do you get your ideas from?'

Of course, the questions are always asked a bit differently, but they're more or less the same.

When Dad first told me about the pre-written replies, I was a bit shocked. I told him it was ungrateful of him – after all, he wouldn't have a job without his readers, the people who actually buy his books. He was silent for a while and then he said, 'Yes, Laureth. You're right.'

He sighed. 'Believe me, it means everything to

get letters like these. But I'm just so busy at the moment . . . '

I still wasn't convinced it was the right thing to do, but the idea of some extra pocket money was too much to resist; I've always got a list of audiobooks that I want as long as my arm, so I agreed.

Oh, and there's a fourth category of emails, which go like this: 'I read your book and it sucked. I mean it really sucked. You're a terrible writer.' Dad's less keen on those.

We don't have a pre-written reply for this category, because Dad says we don't need to reply to people who aren't polite. It makes me angry when I open an email like that. I think Dad's books are really good. Well, most of them. He works so hard on them, and I can't believe how easy people find it to be mean. It doesn't happen that often but the first time I got one it made me want to send a totally nasty message back, but then Dad asked me why I'd want to. What would it achieve? He laughed, an empty sort of laugh, and warned me never to get involved with those sorts of people. He has a friend, another writer, who once replied with a torrent of abuse to an email criticising her novel.

She called the person who'd sent it an illiterate monkey with nuts for brains, only she didn't say *nuts*. It was all over the internet the following week and his friend got into no end of trouble for it. She doesn't get asked to speak at book festivals anymore, for one thing.

Anyway, I was plugging away through the emails as usual, and cutting and pasting Dad's replies, adding a little personal touch on the end here and there if I thought it was a particularly nice email, because I know just what Dad would say, and then I came across one that was different. Very different.

I had VoiceOver turned way up, to almost top speed, so when I heard the subject of the email the first time, I didn't quite catch it.

I fumbled around with the settings on the Mac to slow its speech rate down and then played the subject line again.

*The Black Book.*

That grabbed me at once, because the Black Book is what Dad calls his notebook. He has lots of notebooks, hardback notebooks, always the same, and they're all called the Black Book. He calls them that because they're white, apparently, and apparently that's funny, but I don't really see why.

As I listened to the message, my skin went cold.

The email came from someone called Michael Walker, and he said that he'd found Dad's notebook, and had seen the email address inside the cover and wanted to claim the reward that was offered.

The email finished like this:

*I note that the value of the reward is £50 and so I think I must be right in saying that you're British. I'd like to enquire what the dollar equivalent would be, should I return your book to you.*
*Yours, Mr Michael Walker.*

What made my skin go cold was the word *dollar*. That probably meant America, I knew. Which was odd, to say the least, because Dad was supposed to be in Europe. In Switzerland.

Something wasn't right. Dad's not the most normal of people you could ever meet, that's true. But even for him, this was unlikely behaviour.

I went and found Mum. She was in her bedroom, packing to go to Auntie Sarah's, I guessed.

'Mum,' I said, 'is there anywhere in Europe that uses dollars?'

'Laureth, you're sixteen. You can do your geography assignments by yourself now.'

'Mum, it's the summer holidays,' I said. 'It's not schoolwork. I just want to know which countries use dollars.'

'Why don't you look it up? Google it? You need to be more independent.'

That would have been enough to drive me crazy on any other day. On any other day I'd have been cross, because on the one hand Mum won't let me do anything by myself, and on the other she's always telling me I have to learn to look after myself better because no one else is going to. The fact that she was going to Auntie Sarah's, without us, overnight was something of a miracle in itself, and clearly showed the mood she was in.

'Never mind,' I said.

Then, trying to sound as casual as I could, I added, 'Listen. Where's Dad?'

She sighed.

'Austria. Switzerland. Somewhere like that.'

'When did you last hear from him?'

I hadn't heard from him myself in days. Which was most odd. Usually he's pretty good at keeping in touch, with texts at least.

'Laureth, I don't have time for this.'

She sighed again. I waited.

'About a week ago. Maybe longer. Why?'

'Because he's had an email. Someone's found his notebook. In America.'

Mum didn't say anything, but she stopped moving around for a moment. Then she went on packing.

'I think something's happened to him,' I said. Mum didn't answer.

'Mum, I said—'

'I heard you. Look, it's probably someone playing a prank, that's all.'

'Mum—'

Then she yelled at me.

'Laureth! Just leave it, will you?'

She followed that by going silent on me. I stomped back to the little spare room Dad uses as an office, and after a while I began to think that, well, maybe she had a point. Maybe it was this month's loony email. Dad has a private competition every month for the craziest message, something I'd

32

been happily judging since I'd taken over checking the account.

I sat in front of the Mac again.

I thought about Mum, and then I thought about Dad. I thought about how things used to be and about how they were now. None of this thinking made me feel very happy, so instead I put my fingers back on the keyboard.

I kept it short; no point wasting my fingertips on loonies.

*How do I know you have my notebook?*
*Jack Peak.*

I always sign myself as Dad. It's probably illegal to pretend to be someone you're not but it makes life easier than explaining that I'm his daughter and I'm replying on his behalf. People wouldn't want to know that anyway, they just want a reply from the actual writer.

I sat there trying to think what else to do.

I picked up my phone, wondering whether I'd get in trouble for using it to call Dad. Abroad. It costs a fortune.

Then the email pinged and there was another wordy reply from Mr Walker, but the gist of it was this:

*See for yourself.*

VoiceOver told me there were three embedded images. Attachments.

I swore, then fetched Benjamin. I dragged him into the room and sat him in Dad's chair.

'Don't sit too close,' I warned him.

He made a small grumpy noise.

'I need you to look at something,' I said. 'There are some pictures on this email. Tell me what they are.'

Benjamin sighed, but he did as I asked.

'There's three photos,' he said. 'They're like schoolwork. Writing in a book.'

'Handwriting?'

'Yes.'

'Benjamin, do you think they could be pages from Dad's notebook?'

'Yes. That's exactly what they are.'

'How can you be sure?'

He sighed again.

'Because they have his name. It says "reward offered". There's his email address. Because it's his messy writing. Because—'

'Okay,' I said. 'Okay. Thanks.'

ᙏᘉᚊ

I thought for a long time.

Then I phoned Dad's mobile from mine.

There was no answer, it just kept ringing and ringing.

I went and spoke to Mum again, and told her I was really worried. I told her that I knew Dad was supposed to be in Switzerland doing research for his book, but that his notebook had just turned up in America, and that he wasn't answering his phone.

I could tell things were bad when Mum didn't even have a go at me for calling abroad on my mobile.

'Laureth,' she said, and her voice was hard and thin, the way it often was these days when she spoke to Dad. 'Right now, I could not possibly care less where your father is. Do you understand?'

I wouldn't let it go.

'Mum,' I said. 'I'm worried. I'm worried he's gone missing. Something's happened. If he'd gone to America he'd have told us.'

Mum didn't reply to that.

'He'd have told me.'

In the silence I started to wonder; would he? Would he have told me? I hoped that was still true. Dad might be many things, but he's always texting me and messaging me and as I thought about that, I realised I hadn't heard from him in days. Maybe longer.

'Look, Laureth,' Mum said. 'Stop being so . . . imaginative.'

She said it as if it was a bad word.

'Mum—'

'No, that's enough. You're too much like your father sometimes. Head full of fairy dust. You need to be more responsible, you need to grow up and look after yourself. Be sensible. You're *sixteen*.'

I ignored all that, even though I wanted to say a million things back, but I didn't. Instead, I said, 'Mum. He's gone missing. I know it.'

And she just said quietly, 'And how would we know if he had, Laureth? How would we know the difference?'

I thought again about saying a million things, and sometimes thing is the only word to use. But I was too angry to say any of them, so I said nothing.

My mind was full of two final things; worry, and Dad.

That's when I decided to go and look for him.

## *You Never Know*

When embarking on a manhunt, it's vital to understand the psychology of your quarry. That's what they always say on those detective shows on TV. I thought I had a pretty good grip on Dad's thought processes, but clearly it needed some work. I mean, I know he's a bit strange, but to go missing? That's not Dad. It's just not him. It's more like a story – but then again, fact and fiction, he always says, are hard to tell apart. You never know the difference for sure.

I suppose he would say that, being a writer, but he

says when you've spent long enough making things up to seem as real as you can, it begins to get hard to tell one from the other.

He says lots of authors have said the same thing, over the years, which is why you should never trust the autobiography of a writer; they're just too good at making things up, and more to the point, they're good at believing that what they've made up is *actually* true.

It's when he talks like that that Mum goes quiet, and then Dad says even more peculiar stuff, and usually has another glass of wine or two.

෨෬෬෪

I was thinking about all this when I replied to Mr Walker. I wondered how to ask him if I could trust him without actually saying it. But first I asked him where in the States he was. I got an email straight back.

> *Woodside. That's in Queens if you're unfamiliar with the area. Queens is in New York if you're likewise unfamiliar with that.*

I decided to ask him where he'd found the book.

He didn't reply for a few minutes, and I found myself browsing some airline sites. In my head was a news story I'd heard the week before. A nine-year-old, a young boy from Manchester, had run away from home. He'd flown to Turin before he was stopped. He didn't have a passport, or a ticket. He'd just hung around at the back of a big family group and somehow had got through five separate control points. It was only on the plane when he told someone he was running away that the crew radioed ahead to Turin. Who knows where he might have ended up if he'd kept his mouth shut?

I had no idea if I could fly by myself. I thought it would prove to be impossible, but I was wrong. Being sixteen I was entirely free to fly on my own, without the need to register as an unaccompanied minor. All I needed was a letter from my parents saying I was travelling alone. Five minutes on Pages fixed that.

I stopped myself. There was no way I could do it. I hated to admit it, but it was true. It was one thing to get around by myself at school. That's different. I know where everything is. I know everyone. They know me.

But it's not the real world.

I waited for a reply from Mr Walker, and while I did, I read the section about 'younger passengers'. I'd put headphones on because I didn't want Mum to come down the corridor and hear what I was reading, even though that was unlikely. She never comes into Dad's study unless it's to get me off the computer. She says I spend far too much time on it. She's probably right.

I couldn't quite believe it, but it seemed that it was also fine for Benjamin to fly, as long as he was with someone over fifteen.

My heart began to bounce about in my chest then, because there was one last possible obstacle. But though I read and read, and searched in all the ways I could, for *disabled*, and *impaired*, and *accessibility* and so on and so on for something that meant I wasn't allowed to fly by myself, there was nothing. Nothing to say I couldn't, although there was nothing to say I could either.

It seemed to be what's called a grey area, so there and then I decided to take Benjamin and walk straight into that peculiar mixture of what I'm told is black and white.

I wanted Dad's notebook. I knew he'd be desperate if he lost it. He once lost it for ten minutes and you would have thought the world had ended. It's because it's full of *gold*, or that's what he calls it, anyway.

*I've had a new idea*, I'd heard Dad say to his editor, Sophie, more than once.

*Any good? she'd asked, laughing. Worth much?*

*Gold dust. Gold dust and diamonds!*

And although they joke about it, it's a serious matter to Dad; because he says you can't remember ideas when you first have them – you have to write them down. And when you do write them down, it helps you to see if they're any good or not. If he'd lost his notebook, I hated to think what he'd be like.

So I wanted to get the book back for him so he wouldn't be upset, but more than that, I wanted Dad. And if Mum didn't care if he was missing or not, I did. She'd told me to grow up, be more responsible. And that's just what I was going to do; take responsibility for finding Dad, when she wouldn't even listen to me.

Mr Walker replied again and said he'd just found the book; that was all.

43

We swapped a few mails. I did some sums, looked at some flights. Then I told him I'd meet him at two the following afternoon, and could he please suggest where.

*Very good. I suggest we meet at Queens Library.*
*21st Street, Long Island City.*
*Where are you coming from?*
*How will I recognise you?*

I ignored the first question and instead told him he'd recognise us pretty easily. I'd be wearing sunglasses, I'd have a seven-year-old boy with me and the seven-year-old boy would have a large fluffy raven in his right hand.

៳៷

Mum went to bed early, and when she had, I sneaked downstairs and took one of her six, yes, *six* credit cards from her bag, where she always leaves it, on top of the fridge.

I didn't actually need the card to buy the plane tickets. Like I said, I've learned the numbers off by heart. It's all part of her plan to help me stand on my own two feet, as she puts it. So I know not only the pin numbers for every one of her bank cards, but also the long number, the expiry date, the security digits, everything. So I didn't need the card online, but I knew I'd need it to get some cash when we got to the airport. Fortunately Mum always puts the same one back in the same slot in her purse, because she's very neat that way, so I chose the one I thought she uses the least.

I hurried back upstairs and tucked it into the case of my phone.

I crept into the office and bought two single flights to JFK. They cost a fortune and as I reached the payment page I felt slightly sick, but then I remembered what Mum had said the night before and I clicked the confirm button so hard I almost broke the keyboard.

Just before I went to bed, I called Dad again. It was eleven, so that meant it was six p.m. in New York. He should have been awake. He should have answered. He should have picked up the phone and said 'Laureth!' with his usual laugh, but he didn't. The phone just rang and rang, and then went to Dad's voicemail.

I left him a voicemail; *Hi Dad. It's me. Please, Dad.*
*Call me as soon as you get this. Love you.*

Then I sent him a text message. I said exactly the
same thing.

ᘉᘓᘂ4

My only fear was that Mum would notice the missing credit card in the morning. I lay in bed, nervously
listening to her get ready.

Then she tapped on my door and came in to say
goodbye.

I pretended to be asleep.

'Laureth?' she whispered.

'Mum?' I said, rolling over, trying to sound as if
I'd just woken up. 'What time is it?'

'I'm off now . . . '

'Okay, Mum.'

I waited for her to close the door, but next thing I
knew she was perching on the edge of the bed.

'Listen, Laureth. I'm sorry. Sorry about last night.
I didn't mean to snap at you.'

I felt her hand on my shoulder.

'That's okay, Mum.'

'Yes, well. It's not okay. It's not your fault.'

'What isn't?'

She didn't answer, but I knew she was thinking about Dad. She took her hand away.

'Are you cross?' she asked.

'What about?'

'That you're not coming to Manchester.'

'Oh, no,' I said. 'That's okay.'

I meant it. Mum had explained that Auntie Sarah's party was a grown-up party, so Benjamin and I couldn't go. Any other time that might have bothered me, but to be honest, I was glad not to have to go and pretend to get on with my cousins. They don't like me and they're mean to Benjamin too.

'So what's wrong?' Mum asked.

'I told you.'

'What, dear?'

'I'm worried about Dad. I think something's happened to him. Why else is his notebook in America when he's in Europe?'

'Laureth . . .'

'No, Mum, I mean it. Don't you think we should do something?'

I thought Mum would soften up. That she'd hold my hand and tell me she was worried too, and we'd call the police or something and they'd find Dad and everything would be fine. Then I wouldn't need to go through with my plan.

'Laureth,' she said. 'I think it's your dad that needs to do something. Not us. Not me.'

'But . . .'

'I'll see you tomorrow night, Laureth. Make sure Benjamin eats properly.'

She left the room and closed the door. I heard her go into Benjamin's room. She didn't say anything but I knew she was kissing his messy hair, something he would have squealed about if he'd been awake. The door closed again, and then she went, off to Manchester for Auntie Sarah's party.

∽∾

I waited two minutes, got dressed, and packed a bag. Our passports were where Mum always leaves them. As I said, she's very organised, something that makes my life much easier. When Dad's around it gets harder, because the TV remote is never where you left it, or the telephone handsets, or, in fact, anything.

I checked my phone. There were no texts. No missed calls.

Then I got Benjamin up. He was grumpy at being woken.

'Mum said I didn't have to get up today. She said we're not going swimming.'

'We're not,' I said, and while I packed a bag for him, I told him we were going to America to find Dad.

'Come on,' I said. 'We have to be quick.' I knew we were supposed to check in a long time before the flight, and although Heathrow's only a dozen stops from ours, I knew we couldn't afford to waste time.

Benjamin started to moan a bit, but I distracted him by telling him he needed to pack some comics to read on the way, because it was a long journey. He loves comics more than anything, except perhaps Stan, so even the mention of them was enough to get his cooperation.

'Hurry up!' I said, propelling him into the kitchen so I could throw some cereal at him. 'Don't you want to go and see Dad?'

'Yes!' said Benjamin. 'Where is he?'

'New York. I told you. And we're going to see him later today.'

I hardly believed it myself. See Dad. In New York.

49

It sounded as if I was making it up, making it up just to tell myself that I was doing something, that I could do something, even though it was truly impossible. But then, you never know what's true or not, what's impossible or not, unless you try.

# *The Guard Dogs*

'You should have seen her, Bernard! And then I told her she couldn't, not on a Friday, but she didn't want to listen. Oh no, which was her look out, because it was shut till Monday. And . . . Do we have to take our shoes off? So anyway, she says . . . What, and our coats? Why do you have to get your laptop out? What is this, the Third Reich? So then she drove all the way to . . . Oh bugger it, I've left liquids in my bag. What? Yes, liquids, Bernard, liquids!'

I listened to the woman in front of me in the queue for security.

Occasionally Bernard, who, I assumed, was her husband, managed to mumble a quick reply, but he was too quiet for me to hear. And though she was very annoying, her continuous commentary on everything she had to do made things loads easier for me.

'What? Boarding passes? I thought this was *passports*? Isn't it passports?'

I clung on to Benjamin's hand, tighter than before. I told myself it would make him feel safer.

'This is cool!' he said. 'We're really going to America?'

'Shh,' I said. 'Of course we are.'

'I'm hungry.'

'You've had breakfast.'

'That was ages ago.'

'Miss?'

That was someone else's voice. The woman in front of me had vanished.

'Come on, love,' said a voice a way behind me, and I knew people were glaring at my back.

I held out our passports, with our boarding passes tucked inside.

Benjamin gave me a tiny tug on my hand, which

meant, further forward, so I shuffled a bit and heard a man sigh.

'Just the boarding passes.'

I dropped Benjamin's hand and slid the slips of card from the passports, and held them out.

'Trying to be clever, are we?'

'No, I . . .'

I guessed what he meant. I held my arm even further out and felt the passes snatched away from me.

There was silence. Just the noise of the airport all around; announcements, people's voices, machines buzzing and security alarms beeping somewhere ahead of us.

'Take your glasses off, please,' said the man. He said *please* in that way people do when they really don't mean it.

I didn't want to, but I took my sunglasses off.

Then he said, 'look into the camera.'

I panicked.

'Benjamin . . .'

'Look, we haven't got all . . .'

I heard the man's voice change direction, and then stop as he looked at me.

'What's wrong with you?'

'There's nothing wrong with her,' said Benjamin, angrily.

'Shh, Benjamin,' I said, loving him for being on my side but at the same time cringing in case he made things worse. I tried to move him away from the man, away from his equipment. The last thing I wanted now was for the Benjamin Effect to strike.

The man ignored him anyway.

'What's wrong with your eyes?' he said. 'Just look into the camera, will you?'

I didn't. I couldn't.

'What's wrong with you?'

That was it. Too much. Tears started to come and I snapped.

'There's nothing *wrong* with me,' I said.

Then there was another voice. A passenger behind me. He had an old voice, dry and deep, and I heard him move beside me.

'Now come on, can't you see the young lady is visually impaired?'

'She what?' said the guard dog.

'I'm *blind*,' I said. 'Blind. And I don't know where your stupid camera is. Okay?'

54

There was a long silence from the guard dog, and a whole big bunch of muttering and whispering behind me. My cheeks started to burn, and I flailed for Benjamin's hand.

'Well, what about him?' the guard dog said.

'He can look into your camera if it makes you happy.'

'Are you *allowed* to be travelling?'

Then the nice gentleman next to me got cross. I mean I think he was actually cross on my behalf, and gave the guard dog an earful about discrimination and rights and customer service and I don't remember what else.

The guard dog seemed to panic then, he wanted to get rid of us as fast as possible.

'Could you do that all the time, please?' I said to the man who'd stuck up for me.

Suddenly we were through, and whoever he was helped me get Benjamin through the scanners, where there was another set of guard dogs only a bit less scary than the first. The man told us that we had to take liquids and metal stuff out of our bags, and he even waited on the other side until we were all done.

'Can I help you any further?' he asked.

I turned to his voice. I know people feel weird if I don't pretend to look at them when I speak to them.

'I meant what I said,' I told him. 'People aren't always as kind as you . . .'

I stopped. He didn't need to know, I was sure of that. He'd done more than his good deed for the day, and his help was way nicer than what I often get when I'm out in public.

Second gate passed, I thought, the guard dogs were dealt with. I reached for Benjamin's hand.

'Can we have breakfast now?' he asked.

The man laughed and said goodbye.

'Second breakfast, you mean,' I told him.

'Second breakfast, then,' he said. 'Can we?'

ᗰᑎᕊ

We found somewhere to eat, and that was quite easy. Benjamin started to read me the menu but I always have the same thing in Café Rouge anyway.

Benjamin made sure Stan was eating too.

'It's a long flight to American, isn't it?'

'America,' I said, correcting him. 'Yes. Do you remember?'

'No. I was tiny.'

'You still are.'

'Don't be horrible,' he said, and I apologised.

'It was only two years ago,' I said. 'Not even that.'

I remembered the trip. New York, two years ago. Dad's fortieth birthday. The four of us.

'Why is Dad in American . . . America?' said Benjamin.

'He's working on a book,' I said. 'I think.'

'What book?'

'*That* book,' I said.

'Oh,' said Benjamin. 'Yes. That book.'

ᘛᘚ

Maybe I should mention *that* book.

Dad had been working on *that* book for a long time. A very long time.

That's why I knew about such strange things as numinosity when I was twelve, and apophenia when I was thirteen, and a whole lot about these crazy men with funny names like Jung and Pauli. It all happened in the car, on our journeys to and from school.

When Mum picks me up, which isn't so often, we talk about school, and  lessons, and food. Things like that. She likes to hear that stuff, but if I try and tell

57

her about my friends, like about how Robert's sight is still getting worse, she changes the subject. Usually to clothes. That winds me up a bit because I know why she does it. It's because she used to do it a lot when I was little, teaching me about clothes and making sure I keep myself clean and brush my hair so I always look nice. Funnily enough, I can do that myself now, but she still seems to think I'm eight and have food down my front all the time. I guess it's only because she cares, and besides, it was Mum who taught me that jeans are good because jeans go with everything, and that's very useful stuff to know.

So we natter away about clothes and TV and so on when I'm in the car with Mum, and by the time we get back I feel I've caught up on home life again.

With Dad it's different. It's almost like he's not interested in me at all, and you might think I'd hate that, but I don't, because I get to just listen to him, and talk to him, and he talks to me as if I'm much smarter than I actually am, which has the strange effect of making me feel a bit smarter than I am.

I loved sitting next to him in the car when I was little. I could feel him next to me and smell that smell that was a mixture of the old wool coat he had, and him. And ever since I was little, when Dad picks me up, he tells me about what he's working on, the ideas he's going to use and cool things he's read about.

When I was younger, I know he had one book published every year, and people liked them a lot. He wrote funny books, and I know they sold well because he told me so, and because we used to have really nice holidays. Mum loves her job but being a nurse is not well paid, which I don't understand. It must be tough to do it properly, so she ought to get more than she does, I think, but Mum told me I was naïve when I said that.

If Dad's writing's not going so well, we tend to hang out at Granny's in Cumbria, which is nice too, or at Auntie Sarah's, which is not so nice, because of my cousins.

So after a few years, Dad wrote a really different book. It was called *The Fifth Gate*, and it was different because it was more serious, he told me. He wrote another one after that. I know they didn't sell well because he didn't tell me so.

Mum kept saying he should write the funny books again, but Dad said he didn't want to. He said he didn't feel funny anymore, he said he wanted to write serious books. Mum said they weren't *serious*, they were *miserable*, and then there was a seriously big argument which still makes me hurt if I think about it, so I try not to.

Dad started travelling more after that. Looking for things to write about that would make good stories, even though we didn't have as much money as we used to. Mum and Dad stopped talking about his writing; or if they do, I've not heard them, anyway.

It still gets to Dad, the business about his old books. All the time, when he meets people, and they realise who he is, they say the same thing.

'Oh, oh yes,' they say. Then there's a pause of about four seconds. 'Yes, I like your earlier books. The funny ones. They were great.'

It's a miracle he hasn't killed anyone. Yet.

And then, Dad had an idea for a new book, which he said was neither funny, nor serious. I didn't understand what he meant by that.

'What's it about?' I asked.

We were in the car on the way home from school. Term had ended and he'd come to pick me up for Christmas.

He always says the same thing when he picks me up. He comes to my room, where I'll have been waiting for him. I'm usually the last to go because Dad is always late, so I'm always worrying that something has happened, and then I hear footsteps outside and I know it's him.

'Shall we?' he says.

And I always say the same thing back.

'Why not?'

Then we laugh and Dad carries my bag and holds my hand and we get into the car for the ride home.

And this particular time he told me about his new idea.

'Well,' he said, 'It's about coincidence.'

მჯ4

Mr Walker had emailed me pictures of three pages, and I'd forwarded them to my email and saved them on my phone. One of them was the inside front cover, the bit that talked about the reward and so on. The others were some of Dad's pages of notes about coincidence, and while we had second breakfast, I got Benjamin to read it to me.

# THE FIRST PAGE

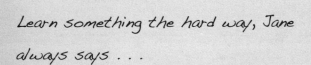

Learn something the hard way, Jane always says . . .

Learn something the hard way and you won't forget it.

In which case, I ought to remember this stuff till the day I die. My brain is starting to melt.

So, a quick recap:

Coincidences: a coincidence is when two or more things happen or occur together even though there

seems to be no CAUSE for them to
do so.

They are much misunderstood.
So . . . :

Maybe there should be
some sections explaining
PROBABILITIES?

Some coincidences that seem
remarkable ONLY DO SO because
most people do not understand much
about MATHEMATICS.

* * *

REMEMBER
BENJAMIN'S
BIRTHDAY

Use, for example,
the Birthday Problem:

You're at a party and you meet

someone with the same birthday as you. Pretty amazing coincidence you say to each other. You laugh about it. You tell your wife; Hey, come over here! This guy has the same birthday as me! Cool huh?

All the way home you have that nice little feeling you get when a coincidence happens to you.

But should you really be so amazed?

PICK UP LAURETH ON FRIDAY :)

If you were to do the maths, you could work out for yourself that you only need 23 people in a room for there to be a better than fifty-fifty chance that two of them share the same birthday.

Given that it's a pretty stinky party that has less than 23 people at it, this kind of thing must happen all the time.

In a classroom of 30 students, you might be amazed if the teacher gets you all to call out your birthdays, and you find two of you have the same one. But the way the maths works means that with 30 students there's around a 70% chance that this is true. With 57 people in the room, the chance is a coincidence-busting 99%.

Not so amazing after all.

It's all about probabilities.

There's even a name for it; Littlewood's Law, after a professor at Cambridge. Professor Littlewood defined a miracle as something that might have a one-in-a-million chance of happening. And then he worked out that given the huge number of events that a person experiences on a daily basis, you can expect to see something miraculous happen once every 35 days or so.

Which means that what appears to be a miraculous coincidence is actually rather ordinary.

# The Stray Book

What Dad meant was this: he was trying to say that perhaps not all coincidences are that amazing. That you only need a little understanding of probability to see that sometimes it's just a question of maths, and not a question of anything freaky going on.

Benjamin went back to feeding Stan and I thought about when Dad had first told me that thing about birthdays. It was ages ago, I was probably still struggling at primary school and I wasn't getting on great with anything, let alone mathematics that were way too hard for an eleven-year-old.

But I understood now.

I tried to get Benjamin to read it to me again, but he moaned and said it was hard, so I left it. He's a good reader for his age, but I was having to zoom in and all around the photo Mr Walker had sent, since I didn't dare let Benjamin touch my phone. If anything happened to it I knew I was in big trouble. So I was pinching and zooming where Benjamin told me to, but it was slow and frustrating getting it right. On top of that, Benjamin said the photos were a bit fuzzy. And then there were some pretty long words in there, but then that's Dad for you; he does seem to like using long words when short ones would do just fine.

Although Benjamin struggled a bit with 'probabilities', he knew 'coincidence', since Dad had been banging on about it for probably almost all of Benjamin's life. Though Benjamin still prefers to call them 'co-inky-dinks' because he found it hard to say when he was younger and it kind of stuck.

Coincidences had become Dad's *thing*. So when we talked about *that* book, that was all we needed to say.

*That* book that wouldn't get written. *That* book that seemed to have stopped Dad from writing anything else. *That* book that meant Mum would rather go to Auntie Sarah's party in Manchester than worry about whether her husband had gone missing.

To be fair, she had a point. Dad was not himself, even he admitted it, and Mum wasn't the only one who wished he'd just give up on *that* book and write something else instead. Preferably something funny.

I remember way back, Dad announced over dinner that he had made an important discovery. Given that he'd probably been working on *that book* for so long already, I think we were expecting something pretty spectacular. A really rather groundbreaking announcement, but what we got was this: the reason, Dad said, that he was having trouble writing about coincidence, was that it was a very hard thing to write about.

He stopped and waited. In the silence, Mum said, 'That's it?'

'That's quite a lot,' Dad said, already sounding defensive. He spoke quickly and his voice was a little higher than usual.

'Listen,' he said. 'It's like this. There're two

reasons why writing about coincidence is impossible. First, think about when a coincidence happens to you. It feels pretty incredible, doesn't it? You get that shiver down the back of your neck, and you think to yourself, what does it mean? That's the point, isn't it? It feels as though it has to mean something. And it feels incredible, so you turn to the nearest person, and you tell them, and they have that look in their eye, and they say, in a really flat voice, "Yeah. That's amazing." And then they change the subject as fast as possible.'

'What look?' I asked. 'What look in their eye?'

'Oh, well, it's hard to say,' Dad said. 'They sort of look over your shoulder, not into your face, and you can just see what they're thinking.'

'You can see what they're thinking?'

'Not literally, Laureth,' Mum said. 'He just means you can see they're not impressed. There's no reaction on their face.'

'Yes, that's it, Jane,' said Dad. He sounded calmer. 'That's just it. There's no reaction. It doesn't mean anything to them, because it didn't happen to them. And usually it sounds pretty lame. I mean, say you're on the way home and you're thinking about salmon.'

'Salmon?'

'Salmon, Manchester United, the moon landings. Quadratic equations. Anything, but let's say you're thinking about salmon. And then just as you're thinking about it, you drive past a huge advert with a picture of Scotland and there's a salmon leaping out of a river.'

'Yeah,' said Mum. 'That's amazing.'

'I know it's not,' said Dad, irritably. 'That's my point. If it happens to you, it seems cool, but you tell anyone else about it, and . . . '

'They're not impressed,' I said. 'So why does that make it hard to write about?'

'Like I said, two reasons. First, because it's impossible to get anyone else to feel the way you do when the thing happens to you. It might not sound impressive to anyone else in real life. So it's sure as hell not going to seem impressive on the pages of a book. No tingles up the back of the neck.'

No one said anything. I was thinking about what Dad had said and Benjamin was stuffing his face and chatting quietly to Stan.

'So that's one thing,' Dad said. 'So then, what do you do? In order to make your reader think your coincidence is cool, you exaggerate it. You make it a whopper. Huge, extravagant, and very, very unlikely to have happened. You see a salmon while thinking about a salmon while sitting next to a man whose name is Salmon who works for the Alaskan Salmon Foundation, and is wearing salmon-coloured trousers. So what does that do for you?'

'I don't know,' I said.

'I don't care,' Mum muttered. I think she was trying to be funny. Dad didn't take it well.

'I bloody care,' he said. 'What it does for you, is absolutely the opposite of what you wanted. You're trying to impress your reader, and what happens is the reverse. Why? Because ludicrous coincidences are well known by everyone to be what terrible writers use to get themselves out of problems with their plot.'

'Oh,' I said.

'Yes,' said Dad. 'Oh. Coincidences in fiction just do not work. And even in real life, they tend to fall into two sorts. The ones that are so pathetic that they don't excite anyone but you, and the ones that are so incredible that they are literally just that; unbelievable. Even to members of your own family.'

'Oh God,' sighed Mum. 'Here we go.'

I could hear that Dad was looking towards Mum when he said that last bit, and I knew why.

What started him wanting to write about coincidences was because one happened to him. I suppose it was one of the second sort; the sort that is so amazing that even your own family doesn't believe it.

Well, I believed it. Mum didn't.

When I was tiny, Dad said he'd been on a train from Manchester to Leeds, and he was reading a book. He was so engrossed in the book that when he got to his stop, he almost missed it. He panicked and got all his stuff together and jumped off the train before it moved on, and he realised he'd left the book on the seat.

Fast forward about five years, and he was on another train – the Eurostar to Paris, going to a book fair or something for a couple of days. On the way out, he sat next to an elderly German lady. He said they didn't speak much, but he offered to get her something from the restaurant car as she was quite frail, and she said please could she have a bottle of water.

Two days later, when he was coming home from the book fair, he got on the Eurostar, and was wandering along the carriage trying to find his seat number. He was looking at his ticket and at the numbers printed above the seats, and then he saw someone a little way ahead, laughing, and smiling.

It was the old German lady, and by chance their seats were next to each other again.

So Dad sat down, and they got chatting about coincidences that had happened to them over the years, so it was only after an hour or so when they stopped talking that Dad went to put his newspaper in the seat pocket in front of him, and saw that someone had left a book behind.

He pulled it out. It was the same book he'd lost on the train to Leeds years before. Not just the same book, I mean, but the *exact same* book. *His* copy, with his name in the front, and his notes in the margins.

At that point, he said he almost fainted, it was so weird. He laughed after a while, and then he got scared for some reason. Scared. He said it actually frightened him. He tried to tell the German lady about it, but she didn't seem to understand what was so amazing.

There was one final thing about this coincidence, which was this: the book that Dad had lost, and then found again while in the middle of another unrelated coincidence, was one of the most famous books written by the great psychologist Carl Jung; his classic work on what he called synchronicity. But which everyone else calls by another name: coincidence.

# The Third Gate

'She doesn't believe me,' Dad said to me in the car one Friday night.

'What? You mean Mum?'

'Yes, I mean your mother,' he said. He was talking about his German-lady-train-book-co-inky-dink. 'I showed her the book and everything. It's a bit much when your own wife thinks you're lying.'

'She doesn't think that,' I said.

'No?' said Dad, and he sounded really fed up.

I'll be honest with you, I wasn't sure that Dad hadn't made that whole story up either, but when he

said that, I believed him. I believed him because Mum
didn't.  I believed him because he needed someone to.
So I did.

〰4

We'd been ploughing our way through second
breakfast for a long time.

'Benjamin,' I said. 'Can you see a screen from
here? With the flights on?'

'Uh-huh.'

'Can you see if our flight is ready? It'll say
something like "Go To Gate".'

'Uh-huh.'

'Don't say uh-huh. It's a bit rude. Say, "Yes,
Laureth, I'd be happy to".'

'Okay, Laureth.'

'Well?'

'Well what?'

'Our flight?'

'Oh. Yes, it says New York JFK. 9:55. Then it
says, "Final Call".'

'Oh crap,' I said.

And then I had to get Benjamin to tell me where
a waiter was so I could pay, and I had to find a

twenty-pound note, and we didn't even wait for change but had to run to the gate which is not something I like to do if it's not somewhere I'm used to, and especially somewhere like an airport full of people.

'Do not let go of my hand,' I said to Benjamin.

'Of course I won't,' he said grumpily, and then I felt bad for making it seem as if I didn't trust him. It wasn't that at all, it was something else, but the something else was not something I could tell Benjamin, because I might have scared him.

And if he got scared, I'd be in trouble.

So I just shut my mouth and we half-ran, half-walked to the gate, and when we got there Benjamin tugged my hand.

'There's people in a queue,' he said.

'You're sure this is 35? For New York?'

'I'm sure, Laureth.'

'Good. Okay.'

We slowed to a walk, and that way we could do the thing that he likes to do and that I like him to do too, where it looks as though I'm guiding him, but actually he's guiding me. A little tug this way, a twist that way. We have it down to a fine art, so good in fact that if I have my sunglasses on, people often have no idea about me. Which sometimes, in fact more than sometimes, is just what I want. People can be so . . . What's the word? Judgemental. Well, that's the polite word, anyway.

There was an announcement.

'All remaining passengers for JFK, please make your way immediately to gate 35. Four minutes until we close the gate. Thank you.'

We got in the queue. I smiled to myself and wanted to tell Dad that the third gate was actually numbered 35, for that would have amused him, and then I tried not to think about Dad. Instead I began to think about what I was doing.

By now, Mum would be halfway to Manchester.

She wasn't due home until Sunday evening, by when, I hoped, we would have found Dad. It was only a matter of hours and everything would be okay. Anyway, it would be way too late to try and stop us. I hadn't left her a note or anything, since we didn't have the time for me to power up Dad's Mac, write a note, print it out, and anyway, even if I had had time, I didn't want Benjamin to read it. I'd decided that I'd text her when we got to New York. Or found Dad.

Suddenly I saw how stupid I was being.

I had no idea if Dad was actually in New York. Just his notebook. Even if he was, I had no idea *where* in the city he was. Where he'd been staying. Or how to find him.

The night before, I'd been angry, angry at Mum for not caring, and angry about that other thing too, the thing I didn't want to tell Benjamin.

Now, in the boarding queue, it was just the reality of standing in line with my little brother, and realising I was being dumb. Irresponsible, in fact.

I pulled my phone out and tried Dad's number. Now it wasn't even ringing. A voice said, 'The mobile phone you are calling is unavailable.' It kept repeating that, over and over, when it should have gone to voicemail.

Then two things happened at once.

Benjamin squeezed my hand, tilting it slightly forward.

'Our go,' he whispered.

And the lady at the desk called me forward.

'Hello? Please come forward.'

So that was it.

I hesitated. I didn't have to say anything, to tell them what was going on. I could just pretend to be ill, or that we were in the wrong queue. In fact, I could just turn and walk away.

Benjamin's hand was hot in mine.

I could simply feel how excited he was.

'Let's go and see Dad, Stan!' he said.

I stepped forward and held out our passports and boarding cards.

I kept my hand held out, which is a trick I sometimes use to make the person put the things straight back in them, so I don't need to wave my arms around looking stupid.

'Have a nice flight,' she said, and we got on the plane.

# The Right Seat

'Deals are made to be broken,' he said, 'which was rich given what . . .'

'. . . when it was more like fifty-four than three!'

'Bernard. Bernard, have you got my cushion? Oh, honestly, Bernard.'

Snatches of conversation came to me as we walked down the aisle of the plane. I often overhear things and like to guess what people are talking about. Sometimes it can be pretty obvious, other times really weird. You hear a little snippet and you wonder what someone can possibly be discussing in order to say 'of course the green ones don't bounce'.

So we were trying to find our seats, when Sam came along, and . . . but maybe I should begin at the beginning.

*Begin at the beginning*, Dad always says. It's one of his favourite sayings, and he likes using it about writing in particular.

It's funny about Dad, and writing, and when I say funny, I don't especially mean hilarious. I mean odd, strange, weird and frequently unpredictable. Sometimes everything is good and he's happy and I think he loves what he does. And then there's the other times when he goes quiet and won't speak about it, and gets grumpy if any of us try to. Then he seems to hate what he does, and I wish he'd give up and do something else instead.

But when it's going well, he's very happy to talk about writing, and how books work, and why some films work and others don't, and stupid ways to write a book. He says writing a book is hard enough as it is without making things any harder, like, for example, writing the middle first and then the end and then a bit near the end, and then the beginning and . . . so on. So, he says, begin at the beginning.

Which, I now realise, I haven't.

I've been jumping about all over the place, but maybe that's because that's how my mind works, whereas Dad thinks in straight lines, connecting the dots, from here, to here, to there. Done.

But maybe there's more than one way to tell a story, maybe you don't have to begin at the beginning, and anyway, who really knows where anything begins?

Dad's favourite example of that is to do with books too. One of the questions he gets asked all the time is how long it takes to write a book. And usually he says 'a year' because it's the easiest thing to say. But occasionally, if he likes the person doing the asking (which I can tell because his voice is warmer) he'll give the real answer. Which is, who knows?

How long does it take to write a book?

Is it the length of time you are banging away on your computer's keyboard?

Does it include the months of changes your editor asks you to make?

Should it be measured from when you had the very first thought that went into it, whatever it was that set you thinking about it?

And does that depend on everything that's happened to you since, well, since you were born?

Is that how long it really takes to write a book; your whole life?

All I knew was that Dad had been trying to write a book for longer than *Benjamin's* whole lifetime, more or less. One day, not so long ago, Mum said he was obsessed. I shouted at her when she said that, because it's not true. It can't be, it mustn't be true.

ᷓᵷᷔ

'There they are,' said Benjamin.

He was ahead of me, walking down the aisle. I remembered how big the plane was the last time we'd flown to America; it seemed to go on for miles, and I'd already bumped into three people.

The aisle was too narrow for us to walk side by side, and I was shuffling along behind Benjamin with my hand on his shoulder. Despite this I'd managed to kick someone's foot and bump elbows with someone else.

I was doing my very best not to look blind, because I was still very nervous about someone finding some regulation, some rule that would get us thrown off.

I just wanted to get as far as being in the air, I told myself, and then I would relax.

So then I knocked into someone else, a woman, who said, 'Why don't you take your oh-so-cool glasses off and you might be able to see where you're going?'

Just like that.

I told her I was sorry, kept my head down, and we moved on. Then Benjamin stopped walking at last.

'35 D, that's you,' he said. 'Oh . . . '

He sounded disappointed.

'What is it?' I asked.

'I wanted a window seat.'

'I'm sorry. We booked so late. I guess this is all there was left.'

'You're here, by the alley.'

'The aisle,' I said, automatically.

'The aisle,' said Benjamin. 'And I'm next to you.'

He put my hand onto the back of my seat so I knew where it was.

'Can you put our bags away?' I asked Benjamin.

'I can't reach,' he said, and then a man's voice said, 'Can I help you with those?'

'I can't reach,' said Benjamin.

'So I see,' said the man. His name was Sam but

we didn't know that yet. He had an American accent.

'You're tall!' said Benjamin.

The man called Sam laughed.

'There you go. I think I'm in the middle too. Next to you.'

He was talking to Benjamin, as he squeezed past me and got into his seat. Benjamin followed him and then I sat down, relieved not to be in anyone's way anymore.

I sent Dad a text. I said the same thing as before: *Please call me. As soon as you get this. Lxx*

I was praying he'd call right back. Then and there. There was still time for him to explain everything and for us to get off the plane, go home, and start begging Mum not to kill me.

Then I was thinking about times, about how long it would take to fly to New York, about the time difference, about when I'd said we'd meet Mr Walker, and stuff like that, and then I heard them announce that the cabin doors were shut, and that we had to turn off our phones.

A few minutes later the plane began to move.

I listened to the bubble of chatter around me, audible above the hum of the engines, and I felt the plane turn and the hum became a roar and we were hurtling down the runway.

I love flying, but I've only done it a few times. There was when we went to New York before, of course, and I've been away with school a couple of times; we even went skiing last Christmas. I love skiing even more than I like flying. The speed was wonderful, the cold air on my face, but best of all I liked the freedom of being out on the slope, with no one holding my hand, no tables to jump out at you, no kerbs to trip over, just the instructor behind me, shouting 'turn!', 'turn!', 'turn!'

The plane thundered on, and I heard the wheels go quiet and felt it tip up into the air, and there was the great feeling of being pushed down and back into your seat.

So that was it.

No turning back, and too late for them to throw us off the plane.

In seven hours, we'd be in America.

# The Plane Trip

With a cheer, Benjamin chuckled as the plane took off.

'Like flying?'

It was the man sitting next to him.

'It's okay,' said Benjamin. 'Stan doesn't like it, though.'

'Stan?' asked the man.

Benjamin didn't say anything. I guessed he was holding Stan up for the man to see, because he said, 'Oh, I see. Stan. Great name for a raven.'

'You're clever,' said Benjamin.

The man laughed.

'You think so?'

'I think so,' said Benjamin. 'Most people think he's a blackbird.'

'Really? People are dumb, aren't they?'

Benjamin didn't answer that, and I hoped the conversation might be over, but it seemed it wasn't.

'So why are you cheering if Stan hates flying?'

'I'm cheering because we're going to see Dad.'

'Benjamin,' I said. 'Leave the man alone. He doesn't want you nattering for seven hours.'

'Oh I don't mind,' said the man.

I do, though, I thought. The last thing I wanted was Benjamin telling the world what we were doing.

'And you must be Benjamin's mum?' the man said.

Benjamin laughed.

'Did I say something goofy?'

'She's my sister.'

'Sister? Oh, hey.'

I tried to work out if he had been joking or not, but I couldn't. Dad's tried to explain to me loads of times how people use their eyes to change the meaning of what they're saying. I just don't get it, but I know it makes it harder for me to spot sarcasm. Irony.

And I know, with my big sunglasses on, and when my hair hangs over my face, which I usually let it, and because I'm quite tall, that people often think I'm older than I am. So he might have made a genuine mistake, or then again he might just have been being a smart arse.

'I'm Sam,' he said. 'Nice to meet you.'

'Laureth,' I said, feeling uncomfortable.

There was a pause and I had that awful feeling I get when I know I'm missing something.

I felt Benjamin grab my wrist and he plonked my hand into Sam's.

'Sorry if I've offended you,' he said. His voice had gone a little flatter than before, and then I felt bad because he'd been holding his hand out to shake mine and I must have looked as if I was ignoring him.

'No, no,' I said, 'not at all. Just distracted, that's all.'

'Scared of flying?'

'No, I love it.'

'I didn't catch your name. Laura, was it?'

'No, Laureth.'

'That's an unusual name. Where's it come from?'

So then I had to tell Sam the whole story about Laureth. Why I haven't learned to say 'it's Welsh,' or something, I don't know. Like Dad does with questions he gets too often. Me, on the other hand, for some reason I feel compelled to tell the whole story.

'My Dad made it up,' I said. 'Well, sort of.'

'Sort of?'

'When I was born Mum had had a hard time, and she was ill afterwards. It was all a bit tough, I think. I was born premature. Really premature . . . '

'That's why she can't—'

'Benjamin!' I snapped. I knew what he was about to say. I must have sounded horrible, but he mustn't say it, I knew he mustn't.

I forced a laugh.

'Always interrupting stories,' I said.

'I am not!'

I paused.

'Anyway, Mum said to Dad that he could choose a name, anything at all, because she was too tired to think about it, and if a writer couldn't choose a good name then what was the point of being married to one?'

'Your Dad's a writer?'

'Uh-huh,' said Benjamin.

'Benjamin,' I said, warningly.

'He is,' said Benjamin, quickly. 'His name's Jack Peak. Have you read his books?'

I loved how proud he sounded. Sam was quiet for a second, as if he was thinking.

'Peak? Jack Peak . . . Didn't he write The Fifth Gate?'

'Yes,' I said.

'Oh yeah. Yeah. But I liked his earlier books. The funny ones.'

'Most people do,' I said, before Benjamin could say anything.

'So he made up the name? Laureth?' asked Sam.

'No, he found it.'

'How do you find a name?'

'In this case, on a shampoo bottle. It's from one of the ingredients; Sodium Laureth Sulphate. He thought it was a beautiful word and sounded like a name.'

'He's right.'

'Mum didn't think so. He swears he told her at the time where it came from, and maybe he did but she was too ill to remember. I was seven when she found out and then she hit the roof. "You named our daughter after a chemical!" That kind of thing.'

'I still think it's a cool name,' said Sam, and I could hear the smile in his voice. It was a soft voice too. I liked it.

'And very beautiful,' he added.

'Thank you,' I said, feeling a little warm inside.

'And that's why I have such a boring name,' said Benjamin.

'Oh, hey,' said Sam. 'That's a cool name too.'

'No it's not,' said Benjamin. 'There are two Bens in my class. Mum said she was going to choose my name when I was born. Dad wasn't allowed. So I got a boring name. But that's why Stan's called Stan.'

'Because you wanted him to have a boring name too?'

'Stan's not a boring name. It's short for Stannous.'

'Stannous?'

'Stannous Chloride,' I said. 'It's a chemical. It was on a tube of toothpaste.'

Sam laughed.

'Mum hit the roof,' said Benjamin, proudly.

ᒧᒥᒷ

We chatted for a bit, and every time the conversation went anywhere near why we were going to New York, or Dad, I steered it away again as fast as I could. Sam turned out to be a student. I thought his voice was young but it's sometimes hard to tell. He'd been in London for a few weeks having a holiday and now he was heading home to somewhere called Riverhead to spend the rest of the summer with his folks, as he called them.

He was studying English Literature, which is cool because that's what I want to study. If I can get to university, I mean.

I could tell Benjamin was getting bored, and I felt bad, but I was enjoying talking to Sam. I was talking about lots of things but avoiding others, and he was asking all about me, about where I went to school, so I told him about King's College, and I must have mentioned my room.

'You go to boarding school?' he asked, and then I tried to change the subject because although King's College is a boarding school it's not the usual kind and I didn't want to get into that. I asked him where he went to university and so on, and then I think Sam guessed that Benjamin was bored too.

'Hey, big guy,' he said, and I decided I was very happy talking to Sam. 'Hey, why don't you watch a film or something? You can play games on here too.'

Benjamin sounded unsure.

'Laureth?' he said, but Sam wasn't listening.

'Sure,' he said. 'Look, you use this control here, or it's touch-screen too. Got it? You press here . . . There. There's all the movies. Like anything?'

'Oh, that's okay,' I said. 'I don't think he wants to watch a film.'

'Yes. I do,' said Benjamin.

'There you go. That's it. You do it. Just press on the film you want. There are some headsets, somewhere, and . . . oh.'

He stopped.

Benjamin made an unhappy squeak, and I knew what had happened. He'd touched the screen.

'That's odd,' said Sam. 'Looks like it's crashed.'

Benjamin went quiet and I didn't know how to stop Sam. He called an attendant and they began to try and fix it. The attendant went away and came back and said everyone else's inflight entertainment systems were working fine, it was just this one.

Then Sam insisted that he and Benjamin swap

seats so he could use his instead, which they did, and then Sam was sitting next to me. I could feel how tall he was from where his arm touched my shoulder. He felt strong, somehow, and he smelled great.

He was just getting Benjamin fixed up to watch some superhero film when they both went quiet.

'That's odd,' said Sam again, and I knew it was no good. The Benjamin Effect had struck.

The next thing was that I heard people's call bells pinging on all around us.

Everyone's systems had crashed. No movies for anyone. Cabin crew came and went trying to calm everyone down and you would think that they were in mortal peril when all that had happened was that they couldn't watch TV anymore. They tried a few times to fix it and then they made an announcement saying that the system seemed to have crashed beyond repair and they were very sorry. There was nearly a riot.

Benjamin was still quiet.

Sam sighed.

'There are these amazing things called books,' he said. 'Never need winding. Maybe these guys could try reading.'

'That's a good idea,' I said. 'Benjamin, would you like your comics?'

Benjamin sounded very fed up.

'Yes,' he said, but I knew what he was really feeling. He was feeling something we all feel once in a while; why me?

# The Fizzy Tist

You should probably know a bit more about my little brother.

Mr Woodell would probably give me a hard time about my vocabulary, but Benjamin has this . . . *thing*. As much as Mum wanted him to have a normal name and be normal too, her wishes were ignored, because although she managed to give him an everyday name, Benjamin has a very weird thing about him indeed.

I feel sorry for Mum, two children and neither of them is 'nice and normal'. After she had me, she must have thought her bad luck was over. She's never once made me feel it, nor Dad. I know they love me. I know they love me as I am, but I know it was hard. It's harder for them than it is for me, because to me, not being able to see is normal. Very few people are born without any sight at all, and I happen to be one of them. I have only the slightest light perception, so I can tell a bright window in a dark room, for example, but that's about it.

I think when the doctors broke the news to Mum and Dad it was a terrible shock. They've never told me that, but my charming cousins have said some mean things over the years. They told me that Mum and Dad wanted to give me up to be adopted. I don't believe that for a second.

My cousins like to do stupid things too, like ask me how many fingers they're holding up, or tell me it's clear to walk through a room and then put something in my way. Once we were at Auntie Sarah's and Mum found me crying, and I think she knew what was going on, but she couldn't bring herself to say it.

So I said it for her.

'It's okay. They're just idiots. Can't handle someone who's a bit different.'

And Mum started crying then and told me how sorry she was but I told her not to be, because you can't miss what you've never had, because I'm not unhappy with the way I am, because I don't mind being blind. What I mind is people treating me as if I'm stupid.

So I know it was hard for them, especially at first, when I was a baby. When I was little.

They'd got used to it by the time Benjamin arrived, and they must have thought everything would be fine. And it is, except for one weird thing; which is the effect that Benjamin has on electronics.

It doesn't happen all the time, but it happens enough for me never to let him hold my iPhone, for example. If he wants to watch TV we have to put it on for him and he has to keep his distance. He can't play computer games, and he's not allowed on the Mac.

It's hard for him, because all his friends play games, and he can't join in, in case the device goes haywire, and then everyone hates him.

It's made him different from other children his age. For one thing, he reads a lot, because books can't crash, and that's good. But it's made him a bit odd too. Most seven-year-olds have stopped walking around with fluffy animals, but ever since Dad brought Stan back from the Natural History Museum in Gothenburg, Benjamin will not be parted from him. Benjamin is a loner; he's ended up that way because lots of other kids find him strange. And I love Benjamin to bits, but I'm away at school during the week, and then he's more or less on his own. So Stan is sort of an imaginary friend, although as Benjamin would be the first to point out, he's not entirely imaginary.

That's how things were, and then, some time last year, Dad was reading a book on the sofa one night and he suddenly roared in delight.

'Benjamin!'

He called upstairs.

'Benjamin! Come down here!'

He was so excited that Mum and I came in to see what was going on.

'I've found something,' Dad said. 'I've found someone else like you! A famous man! He's one of the most famous scientists ever. He was called Wolfgang Pauli, from Austria. A physicist.'

Benjamin was excited too.

'A what?' he asked.

'A physicist is a man who figures out how the universe works, down at the very smallest level. Atoms and things. And Pauli was one of the most important ones, ever. And he had the same thing as you! All through his career, things would break around him. In the lab, at home. Equipment would fail and stuff would break and if he walked into another scientist's lab they'd scream at him to get out!'

'And he was a famous fizzy-tist?' asked Benjamin. Dad laughed.

'The best! Once he was only passing through a town in Switzerland on a train, a town where another scientist was working, and right at that moment the scientist's equipment collapsed! They gave this thing a name; they called it the Pauli Effect.'

Mum and I laughed too.

'There you are then, Benjamin,' she said. 'Now we know what to call it. The Benjamin Effect!'

And that's a weird thing, because just giving it a name made Benjamin much happier about it. Some of the time I even think he's proud of it.

Until he crashes the TV screens of five hundred

people on a jumbo-jet, and then, for his sake, I want him to be just like everyone else, staring at their movie with their headset on, without a care or a thought in the world.

# The Blind Hero

'Might be an idea to have a nap,' I said to Benjamin. 'I want my comic,' he said, grumpily, but I didn't blame him.

Learn something the hard way, Mum says, and you won't forget it. By which she means that if you make a complete monkey of yourself doing something and the embarrassment is almost more than you can bear, you won't do it again. I know what she means, because I had practical examples to follow, from my own experience. Like once when I was young and playing with my cousins I decided

I could do everything they could do. That's why I cycled into a tree and now have a nifty little scar on my forehead.

People sometimes ask me if I want to be able to see, and I say no, I don't. I know they don't believe me but then they ask if I've *ever* wanted to, and I try and explain that it's a meaningless question. It's as meaningless as that other question I get all the time; what colour means to me. I've never known what these things are, so how can I know if I want them or not?

Mum says my scar doesn't look as big as it feels when I run my fingertip over it, and although I hate to admit it, it did make me more careful, that cycling thing. I wanted to go on doing everything everyone else does. But I've never got on a bike since then.

'You won't do that again,' I remember Mum saying. 'Learn something the hard way . . .'

It's an interesting theory but one that requires greater fieldwork and more rigorous testing, at least it does according to my subconscious.

As it turned out, Benjamin had only brought one comic with him.

I'd thrown some underwear and socks in his bag, his toothbrush and some pyjamas too. His clothes were easy to find; thanks to Mum they're always in the same drawer, and since seven-year-olds are not renowned for their fashion sense, I knew he wouldn't mind if his socks didn't match his underpants. His toothbrush is smaller than anyone else's, and he was wearing his pyjamas when I woke him up. So that was all pretty easy. But we were running a bit late by the time we'd finished first breakfast, so we were out of the door and I didn't have time to check what Benjamin had brought with him.

So then came the issue of standing up, finding Benjamin's *Watchmen* bag and fishing out his comics and trying to do all that without giving the game away to Sam, or anyone else watching for that matter.

I'd heard Benjamin's bag thump above my head and I knew there were simple latches in the middle of each overhead compartment. I waited until Sam was asking Benjamin what comics he liked and then

I stroked along with my hands until I found the latch. Benjamin's bag was right there; it's easy to find because there's a big rubber smiley face on the back of it; I can feel the holes for the eyes and the mouth. Mum says Benjamin's too young for *Watchmen* but Dad got the bag at Comicon and it's really rare. I don't know if he gets all of it, but he loves it anyway, and you don't have to understand everything about something to love it, do you? In fact sometimes that can make you love something more.

I fished inside the bag, and found only one comic.

'Is that all you brought?' I said, sitting down and holding the comic out across Sam, hoping I wouldn't punch him in the jaw, but airline seats are very helpful; you know pretty much where everyone is at any given time.

Benjamin practically snatched the comic out of my hands.

'It's a long way to New York, and you only brought one comic?'

'You didn't tell me to bring lots,' Benjamin said defensively.

'I told you it was a long journey,' I said. 'Oh, Benjamin . . .'

I groaned.

There were at least six hours left. One boy, widely known to be a fast reader, and one comic.

'What did you bring, anyway?' I asked.

'Just a . . . comic,' said Benjamin, vaguely.

Benjamin is a huge fan of American comics. He bought his first ones on our trip two years before, when he could barely read. But he loved the pictures and Dad would read them to him. He pretty much learned to read with comics, which is probably why he has such a peculiar vocabulary, and knows words like *radioactive* and *nemesis*. He can probably spell *abduction* too.

'Which one?'

'Just an old one,' he said, and Sam must have seen it too because he started talking to Benjamin again.

'Oh, *Daredevil*! Cool.'

Then I knew why Benjamin didn't want to tell me which one, because he knows it bothers me.

'Have you seen the episodes with Elektra?' said Sam.

'Do you know *Daredevil*?" asked Benjamin.

'Not personally,' said Sam, 'but I've read just about every Marvel comic ever printed.'

So they were off into geek heaven for about half an hour, leaving me to wonder why it is that in books and films and comics there are only two kinds of blind people.

There are the pathetic helpless figures of woe, only in the plot probably because the writer thought it would be really heart-breaking to have a poor blind person not see something terrible happening right under their nose. Sometimes the author seems to go to great lengths to demonstrate that blindness is worse than death. You'd be amazed at the writers who've done that.

Outcomes for this kind of blind character fall into two camps. Either their sight is miraculously restored, hooray! Or they die. *Well at least then they're not blind anymore.*

I blame the Ancient Greeks. They started it. Their stories are full of blind prophets. *They can't see in this world, but they can see in others.*

And then there are the superheroes. Like Daredevil. I saw the film version with Benjamin one Saturday afternoon on TV. I didn't know what it was about and I'm guessing Benjamin didn't to start with, but it's about this man who's blinded by toxic waste, which also enhances his other senses so that he turns into a superhero. He is of course also amazingly handsome and is soon quickening the heart of Elektra.

I went off to my room after half an hour, and left Benjamin to it.

The idea of other senses being enhanced is not unique to Daredevil.

I think people like the idea that if you went blind, your other four senses might become super-powered, but that's not how it is. Well, not for me, at least. I think I pay more attention to the senses I do have. I don't use echolocation like Harry, but I can tell when I'm near a wall, or a bookcase, or something big, just from the way sounds are different.

Anyway, people are wrong when they think we only have five senses. There are lots of others, but for some reason the concept of five seems to be all we ever talk about. Sight, hearing, touch, taste, smell. But there are others, and no, I'm not talking about the sixth sense, ESP, or whatever you want to call it. I'm talking about other senses. Like the sense of balance. The sense of temperature. The sense of the passage of time. The sense of the relative positions of your body parts to each other; that's why you can touch your nose in the dark.

It's why *I* can touch my nose, and I assure you it's not ESP.

So really, people have an amazing set of skills to use, and very useful they can be too, but trust me, if you're blind, your other senses do not help you 'see'.

Take Luke Skywalker. Obi-Wan puts the blast shield on his helmet down when he's training with the Lightsaber.

'I can't see,' says Luke, sounding a little whiny as he so often does.

'Use the Force, Luke,' says Obi-Wan Kenobi. 'Reach out with your mind.'

And Luke knows exactly where to wave his magic wand, but take it from me, there is no such thing as the Force.

There's more unsighted swordplay in a Japanese film about a blind samurai. He kills about fifteen people a minute. I say there's one film; apparently there's dozens of them, I guess because people love this stuff. People are fascinated by the idea of being blind, I've learned that. Fascinated, and scared too. I think that's where the blind hero comes in. *Oh, wow, he's blind but he still kicks ass.*

♏♌

Right then, I can confirm I didn't feel like I was able to kick anyone's ass, but to change the subject to the quickening of hearts, mine was doing just that.

Sam left Benjamin to *Daredevil* and turned back to me.

'There's something cool about you,' he said.

'Really?'

'Yeah, really,' he said, making fun of me. I liked it.

His arm was touching mine on the armrest between the seats. I wondered if he realised that, if he was doing it on purpose.

'And what's that?' I asked.

'I dunno,' he said. 'I don't get you. One minute you're a little weird, and the next you . . . '

He stopped, and I think he might have embarrassed himself.

'What?'

'You turn that smile on me.'

That panicked me. I often worry about the smiling thing. I was getting grief in class last year for 'looking dumb'. That was the chosen vocabulary of Mr Woodell. He told me I looked bored during his lessons.

If you're blind it doesn't really matter if you have your eyes open in class or not. Sometimes I feel I can concentrate better with them shut. But to keep him happy I tried to put what I imagined was a sort of fascinated grin on my face. He told me I looked psychotic. You would think a teacher in a school of blind kids would have got used to it by now, but he's new. I guess he'll give up eventually.

'Hey, now you've gone weird on me again,' Sam said.

'Sorry. I don't mean to,' I said.

'Listen,' Sam said. 'Benjamin tells me you're going to meet your dad in NYC.'

'He did . . . ? Oh, look . . . '

'So I was thinking maybe you might wanna get together with me sometime in the next few days? For a drink?'

I didn't say anything.

I was thinking that there were probably two things he didn't know about me. The first was my age. And the second . . .

'There,' he said. 'You've gone again. Listen, if you don't want to, that's—'

'No,' I said. 'Sorry. I'd love to. Only I'm not sure what we'll be up to and . . . '

'Where are you staying?'

'Oh, I . . . Somewhere, somewhere in the . . . er . . . city.'

There was a silence and I guessed he was thinking I was being odd again, or evasive, or both.

'Do you know where you're staying?'

'We're going to meet Dad,' I said.

'And where's he staying?'

'Somewhere . . . In . . . '

'In the city. Right.'

I thought I'd definitely blown it by then, but Sam said, 'Why don't I give you my number and then if you feel like it, you can call me, yeah?'

I smiled. Then I thought about Mr Woodell, and I toned it down.

'Sure,' I said. I pulled out my phone. 'What's your number? Wait! I have to put your name in first.'

And I guess I was excited because I forgot about my phone. I began swiping and tapping my way through to the contacts, and was just typing SAM into a new contact, when he spoke again.

'Why'd you have your phone like that?' he said, and now he was the one sounding weird.

I froze.

When I use my phone I hold it up flat in front of me so the speaker, which is at the bottom, is easier to hear. Sometimes I use an earphone so no one hears it talking to me, but I was excited. I forgot.

'Well, I . . . '

'Why do you have it talking to you?'

'It's an iPhone,' I said. 'I . . . '

'I have an iPhone too but it doesn't talk to me.'

'But it could do, if you wanted it to.'

'Why would I want it to do that?'

'Well, you might,' I said. 'If . . . '

'If what?'

That was it then. I'd backed myself into a corner. But we'd been getting on really well, and I knew he liked me. He was giving me his number, for God's sake. I chastised myself for being so paranoid. So I told him.

'If you were blind,' I said, quietly.

He said nothing, and I wasn't sure if the penny had dropped. I'd been working my hardest not to seem blind in front of him. I'd turned towards him when he was speaking, I'd even tried nodding when he spoke which is something else Mr Woodell is keen on, though I can't see the point of it. I'd been careful not to touch my eyes, which I do when I get nervous, or scared. So I guessed it was possible he didn't have the slightest clue, despite Benjamin getting me to shake hands with him.

So I took my sunglasses off.

There was a short silence, during which, I suppose, the penny was dropping.

'Oh,' he said. 'Hey. I'm sorry. I had no idea.'

I wondered what he was sorry about.

'That's okay,' I said. I put my glasses back on. 'It's amazing what an iPhone can do. No one seems to know, but that's not surprising.'

'Uh, yeah. No,' said Sam. 'Right.'

'I can type into my phone. It tells me what key I'm pressing and then . . . '

I typed SAM to show him.

'Yeah. Yeah, that's pretty cool.'

'Isn't it?' I said. 'So, what's your number?'

There was a long silence, after which Sam said, 'Listen, Laureth, I'll bet Benjamin's done with

121

*Daredevil* now. He probably wants his big sister back. I need to go to the bathroom anyway, so we can swap back seats. Right, Benjamin? You done?'

'Uh-huh,' said Benjamin. I didn't tell him off.

I let Sam get out to go to the loo, and when he came back he sat in his old seat.

'Hey,' was all he said as he tapped me on the shoulder to get me to move and let him in. He brushed past.

'Thanks,' he added, and then Benjamin snuggled in next to me.

'I'm tired, Laureth,' he said.

'It was an early start, honey,' I said. 'Why don't you curl up and have a little rest?'

He did, and I felt Stan squash up against my cheek as Benjamin used him for a pillow.

I let Benjamin snuggle into me and I felt worried. My mind drifted to a conversation Mum and I had had about him. He's a loner, is Benjamin. He's different from the other boys at school, Mum said, and the Benjamin Effect doesn't help. But that's not the real problem. He's very smart for his age and the other kids think he's odd. He probably is and having a crazy father and a sister who's away a lot of the time probably doesn't help. He worships Dad. He tries to speak like him, uses his phrases if he can. He wants to be just like him.

But then, we all sometimes want to be something we're not, I guess. Mum's tried inviting friends round for tea and so on, but it hasn't really worked. And when I'm not there during term time, Benjamin just sits in his room and reads, and reads, and reads.

'Stan's tired too,' said Benjamin. 'Are you?'

We started to doze, leaning on each other, and I thought about Benjamin for a while, and how he would be when he grew up. Then I wondered a bit about me, and what I would do when I left school. Whether I'd get to university. Whether I could get a job. Whether I'd meet someone, get married. That kind of thing.

And then I thought about Sam, two seats away, and I thought about Mum's theory, that what you learn hardest, you never forget. It definitely needs further thought, that theory, it needs further thought.

'Yes,' I whispered to Benjamin. 'I'm tired.'

But Benjamin was already asleep.

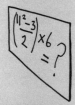

$$\left(\dfrac{11^2-3}{2}\right)\times 6 = ?$$

# WHO KNOWS WHAT?

Love this idea: put it in the book:

What should we make of the birthday problem?

It tells us that it's not so amazing to run into someone with the same birthday as you, doesn't it? Doesn't it show that we should stop getting so excited about coincidences? Because it's all about the maths.

Another school of thought on coincidences goes like this; yeah, sure, amazing things happen sometimes. But there are a lot of people in the world. There are a lot of things in the world. And there are an almost infinite number of ways that these people and these things can come together, by chance, so that occasionally, even the most unlikely things will happen, and when they do, we get all excited and call it an unbelievable coincidence.

Like me on that train from Paris with that German woman and my copy of Jung.

But really, this theory says, it would be more incredible if things like that NEVER happened. That's what would really defy belief.

That's how some people would like us to think about coincidences, and the birthday problem proves it, yes?

No. I don't think it does.

* * *

Think again about the problem. It doesn't show that it's no big deal for YOU to meet someone who has the same birthday as you in a room of 23 people. What it shows is that the chance of ANY TWO people in the room having the same birthday is very high.

But look: every time you meet someone new, the chance you share a birthday with them is only one in 365. And just how often do you even find out someone's birthday? Apart from close friends, I mean. It's not like you walk into

a room full of strangers and say,
'Hey, April 8th anyone?'

Looked at this way, things start
to change. I think it's important to
look at it this way, because if you
look at it the way mathematicians
do, then something very important is
forgotten; and that's the HUMAN
element in all this.

Yes, according to the maths,
half the time in a room of 23
people, two of them will share a
birthday. The maths tells us this,
but the maths forgets that a) we
don't go around finding these things

out, and 6) the maths doesn't
know HOW IT FEELS when a
coincidence happens to you.

Maths doesn't get a tingle up
its neck. Maths doesn't shake
its head and say, Christ-on-a-
bike! But we do. We know how it
feels, and how it feels is that it
MEANS SOMETHING.

There's a word for the
feeling that we are in touch
with something great, something
powerful, something outside
ourselves, and that word is
NUMINOUS. It used only to be
used in connection with religion;

that feeling that you're in touch with God. But not anymore. Nowadays, even atheists use it, when they want to talk about the presence of something mystical and powerful and unknown hovering within our reach.

The numinous experience TELLS us that coincidences mean something.

But who knows what?

COINCIDENCE + NUMINOUS = WOW, MAN!

# The Third Page

The question remained: was Dad obsessed?
He was certainly curious about coincidence, fascinated even. But obsessed?

ᴍᴒᴒᴛ

'What's Sam doing?' I whispered in Benjamin's ear when he woke up.

'Who's Sam?' he said.

'Shh!' I whispered. 'The man you were speaking to.'

'Oh,' said Benjamin. 'He's watching a film on his

iPad and he's gone to sleep with his earphones in.'

So then I got Benjamin to read the third page of the Black Book that Mr Walker had emailed, once again with me holding the phone and zooming and swiping when Benjamin told me to.

In it, Dad was writing more about the thing about birthdays and he talked about the *numinous*. Benjamin stumbled over that one a bit so it obviously isn't used in comics very much, but I knew what he was trying to read because Dad, and then even I, tried to explain to Benjamin what it meant.

I explained it like this: Dad says coincidences mean something to us simply because we *feel* that they do. They must. But I still wondered if that meant they actually *did*.

And then I began to wonder about Dad, and what Mum calls his 'state of mind' when I'm in earshot, but which I know is something he's been taking pills for, because I've heard them arguing about it through my bedroom wall.

The third page that Mr Walker had sent had set me thinking, and there and then I wanted the book and to get Benjamin to read the rest of it to me, as soon as possible.

I tapped my phone to get it to tell me the time.

'Are we nearly there yet?' Benjamin asked.

'Not long,' I said. 'An hour, I think.'

The flight had gone amazingly quickly. What with a couple of meals to navigate and some trips to the loo and making an idiot of myself to cute Americans, time had flown by.

Sure enough, it wasn't long till we were told to prepare for landing.

As I was making sure Benjamin was strapped in properly, Sam spoke to me.

'Er, excuse me,' he said. 'Laureth?'

'Yes?' I said. I tried not to sound cross, because I wasn't, really. I was used to the way he'd reacted, or things like it, at least. And the way he'd changed when he'd found out about me was definitely not as bad as having abuse yelled at me in the street, or having some kid bully me, which happened all the time when I was in a mainstream school; from simple things like hiding stuff from me, to the stuff that can literally hurt like pulling my chair away, to the stuff that's worst of all; being ignored. As if you're not even there.

After all that, it would be very easy to conclude

that people are basically mean, but then there are kind people, like the man in the airport who'd helped us through security. People aren't all the same. There are nice ones and mean ones and all other sorts. Dad says he's only learned one thing in his forty-something years on the planet, and that's this: *people are funny*. And he doesn't mean in the hilarious way either.

For example, there's even bullying at my school, although we're *all the same*. This surprises some people. But we're actually not all the same either; some of us are more blind than others, and in the kingdom of the visually impaired, the kid with partial sight is king. Or something like that.

'Listen, I oughta tell you. It's none of my business, but you don't seem to know where you're going, or where you're staying or where you're meeting your father.'

'Just because—'

'Hey, wait up. I don't care. I think you can handle yourself. But that's not the point. United States Border Control are kind of tough . . . You have to tell them at Border Control where you're staying. Which hotel, and for how long. If you don't know you oughta think of something. You have to put it on your customs declaration.'

I didn't reply for a minute. I guess I must have looked weird yet again, and I didn't want that. I could see he was trying to help.

'Thank you,' I said. 'I didn't know that.'

'Yeah, you need to fill out a customs declaration card. That thing they gave you when we took off.'

Oh, I thought. Is that what it was?

I got Benjamin to find it; we'd tucked it in the seat pocket.

'Listen,' I said to Sam. 'Could you help me fill it in? I'm guessing you might make a better job of it than Benjamin.'

Benjamin started to complain, but Sam laughed.

'Sure,' he said. 'I'd be happy to. We just need to think of a hotel for you to say you're staying in. Don't worry, it won't matter what we put. They never check. Not unless they're suspicious.'

He began to get my details and fill them in on the card. Name, flight number, hotel, that sort of thing.

'Hey,' he said. 'About before. I—'

I stopped him.

'Don't worry about it,' I said. 'Really. It's fine.'

'Why don't you take my number anyway? In case you get in a fix and need something.'

'Thanks,' I said, 'but we're okay. I have Benjamin. We'll be fine.'

'Yes,' said Sam. 'I'm sure of that.'

And then we landed in New York, and before I knew it, everything went freaky, and the last thing I was sure of was that we'd be fine ever again.

## One Blind Girl

Blind I may be, but I think *anyone* could have got lost in the arrivals hall at JFK. The hall sounded enormous, sound drifted to me from a long way to my left and from high up too. In the distance, someone shouted, telling people which queue to get in, only they called it a line.

'Found you!' said Benjamin, grabbing my arm.

As soon as we'd landed he'd announced that he needed the loo again and he'd left me standing in the hall by a pillar.

'Ready?' I asked.

'Uh-huh,' Benjamin said. Then, 'Yes, Laureth.'

'I think there are different queues. For Americans and for us. That's how it was last time. Can you see?'

'It's confusing,' Benjamin said. 'There's thousands of people. They're queuing up for these little glass booths. It's going to take ages.'

'It'll take even longer if we get in the wrong queue. Go and find someone to ask, someone in a uniform. I'll wait here.'

So he did, and while he was gone I started to fret about the time. My phone had changed to New York time already, and we'd landed around half past twelve. I'd arranged to meet Mr Walker in the library at Queens at two, but it was already one o'clock and if the queues were as long as Benjamin said . . .

He came back, grabbed my arm again, and we joined a long and slowly shuffling queue. Neither of us spoke much. We were tired, though we'd both dozed on the flight. I was fingering our passports and our customs declaration card, and with them, in an envelope, I had the letter from Mum and Dad that I'd printed late the night before. I'd had a bit of trouble with that, not writing it – because that'd been easy

– but printing it. The printer wouldn't work and there was no way I could get Mum or Benjamin to help me. For obvious reasons I don't usually use the printer, so I'm not sure about how to use it. In the end I pushed every button on its front and it spewed out the copy I needed. At least I hoped it was, and not something that had been sitting in the print queue for three months. If I handed a copy of Dad's accounts over, we probably wouldn't get very far.

I panicked and showed the start of the letter to Benjamin.

'What's that say?' I asked.

Benjamin sighed. I could tell he was bored, and tired of standing in the queue.

'To whom it may concern . . . ' he began.

'That's fine,' I said. 'Thanks.'

I relaxed, I had the right letter. I was proud of that opening, it sounded very formal and grown up.

And then it was our turn.

Benjamin had described for me what people did when they went up to the glass booths. They stood there for about a minute, he said, and the man (they were all men, he said) behind the desk asked questions. And the person had to put their hand up onto something that he couldn't make out; first one hand, then the other. And then they wandered into the hall beyond where they have those big turntable things that bring your bags back to you.

Benjamin led me to the desk, and I did a little trick of brushing the documents up its side until I felt the edge, and slid them onto the top.

'Business or pleasure?' said a voice. A voice with a big, big New York accent.

'Er, pleasure.'

'Take your sunglasses off while at the desk, Miss, please.'

It was that kind of please, again. It was more like 'or else'.

I did what I was told.

There was silence.

'Look into the camera,' said the man, but I could tell he was looking away from me, probably at a computer screen, trying to find out if we were known terrorists.

'Er,' I said.

Benjamin squeezed my hand.

'It's up to your left,' he said.

Silence. Then, 'Miss, are you visually impaired?'

So that was that.

'Yes,' I said.

'Miss, you're how old?'

'Sixteen.'

'And this is your brother?'

'Uh-huh,' I said.

'Hey!' Benjamin complained.

'Yes,' I said. 'Benjamin is my brother.'

'And you're travelling alone?'

'Yes, but we have a letter from our parents. It's right there in the envelope.'

There was a short shuffling of paper.

'This letter is unsigned.'

I went cold inside. Of course it needed to be signed. It's just not something I've ever done, or would ever think about.

'Oh, well, Mum must have forgotten to, and Dad couldn't have signed it anyway, because he's here.'

'He's here?' said Benjamin, and he tugged my hand as he looked around.

'Whoa, son,' said the man behind the desk. His voice was slightly above me and he sounded very stern. 'You wait right there.'

Benjamin stopped wriggling.

'I mean,' I said, 'he's here, in New York, so he couldn't have signed the letter.'

Then I started to get carried away.

'In fact, he's outside now. He's waiting for us.'

'He's outside?' cried Benjamin.

'Yes, of course he is,' I said.

There was another long silence from the man.

'Dad's here?' said Benjamin.

'Shh,' I said. 'Let the man do his job.'

'The man's talking to someone else,' Benjamin said. 'In the next box.'

And if that was true, he was talking so quietly I couldn't hear him. I tried to look as innocent as possible, which I have no idea how to do. I've been told, countless times, that what freaks sighted people out about blind people is that we simply don't look at anything. We just seem to stare into space. I have struggled a thousand times to understand why anyone would think we would be looking at anything in the first place, and have failed. But I do know it makes people feel uneasy and sometimes even cross, so if it's really important, I do my best to pretend I'm looking at something.

I turned my head to where I'd last heard the man's

voice, and put my best non-psychotic smile on while I waited for him to finish his discussion.

He did, but there was little explanation.

'We're going to ask the supervisor about your status,' he said. Whatever that meant. I guessed it wasn't good. I had visions of sitting in a tiny room being interviewed. Or worse, while they phoned Mum. Or worse still, being put on a plane back home.

'Put your hand on the palm-reader,' he said, then added to Benjamin. 'Son, show her where it is. Right hand first.'

Benjamin helped me find the reader and I put my right hand on it, then my left, while it read my palm. I think it was for fingerprints, not for telling fortunes, but then, I'd already met my tall stranger for the day, and he'd given me the brush-off.

'Now you, son,' said the man, and Benjamin said, 'Cool! I'm James Bond.'

There was a short pause and then man behind the desk groaned.

I heard some tapping of keys, gently at first and then more insistent.

'Shoot,' he said, and I didn't understand at first. 'I'm going to ask you to come around to the next window, to my colleague here. There seems to be a problem with the system.'

'Oh no,' I said, in a small voice.

'Miss?'

'Nothing,' I said. 'Nothing.'

So we were put at the head of the queue next to us, and Benjamin had to put his hand on that reader too, and for a moment I thought everything was okay, but when he put his left hand up, he managed to break that one too.

After he crashed a third machine, there was a whole gaggle of officials around us. People were shouting from the queues asking why desks were closing when the airport was so busy. Guards were telling them very firmly to be quiet or they would be refused entry to the United States of America, and all the time our man and several others were crowding around a fourth desk while Benjamin was told to put his palm on the reader.

My heart was thumping away, and I prayed that the fourth machine might be more robust than the others.

It was.

It appeared to have survived the Benjamin

Effect, and it also appeared that in the chaos, the man had forgotten that we were supposed to speak to someone about why the letter from our parents wasn't signed.

He told us to leave, and Benjamin began to tell them sulkily that their machines were rubbish but I yanked his arm in what I hoped was the right direction.

'Just look for the exit,' I said. 'And don't look back.'

## *One Money Size*

'Girl? You need a ride? Lady?'

A man's voice, so American it was like a movie.

'Low fares!' he said, and I held Benjamin's hand tighter and whispered to him.

'Is that man a real taxi driver?'

'He's got a car,' said Benjamin.

'That doesn't mean he's legitimate,' I said.

'What's that?' asked Benjamin.

'It means he might not be a real taxi driver.'

'Then what is he doing with his car at the airport?'

'Listen . . . '

I was about to try to explain when I heard someone else giving the man a hard time, telling him to move his car along, or they'd call the police. Whoever this second person was then spoke to us.

'Taxi, ma'am? The line is right over here . . . Don't ride with those unlicensed drivers, you hear?'

 ᙢᘁᒎ

So we were in a taxi, heading for Queens Library.

All the business with Benjamin had taken ages, and it was already quarter to two. I felt stupid for not remembering how long it takes to get through US Immigration, but I don't remember the thing with the palm scanners last time, and even if the rest of us had to do it, I guess they thought Benjamin was too young back then and didn't have to.

It was hot. Walking out of the air-conditioned airport gave us no warning of just how hot an August afternoon it was. I got a brief whiff of the heat as the doors slid open, and then it was like walking into a sauna; very hot, and humid. Hard even to breathe.

The taxi was air-conditioned too, and I was glad. I was almost scared by how vicious the heat was, and

I hadn't brought any sun cream, or . . .

'Miss?' the driver said. He hadn't understood me, so I tried again.

'The Public Library in Queens,' I said. 'Main Street, Flushing. Please?'

'Oh, the Queens Library,' he said, and then we were away.

'I thought you said Dad was waiting for us?' Benjamin said, for the fifth time. 'You said he was outside. Why are we getting a taxi?'

'Benjamin,' I said. 'Benjamin, please. Dad's not here, okay. We're going to look for him.'

'But you said he was at the airport.'

'I had to tell that man that. Or he might not have let us through.'

He very nearly didn't anyway, I thought.

'You told him Dad was here,' Benjamin said. 'But he's not?'

'No,' I said. 'He's not. We're going to look for him, remember?'

'Is that where we're going now?'

'Yes. Well, sort of. We're going to meet a man who has Dad's notebook.'

'Why? Does he know where Dad is?'

151

I didn't know how to answer that. I didn't want to lie to Benjamin. It would have been so easy to, but I could never lie to him.

'I hope so,' I said. 'Maybe he does. Hey, how's Stan? Does he like it in New York?'

'He doesn't like how hot it is outside. He can't take his feathers off.'

'But it's cool in here.'

I heard Benjamin chatting to Stan.

'Look, Stan,' he said. 'It's American.'

I was about to correct him when I realised he was right, in a way. It *was* American. I've never felt heat like it at home. Even a couple of minutes of it had left me feeling exhausted. There was a radio on in the back of the taxi, and the voices spoke fast in strong accents, again like they were off the TV. The taxi drove fast, weaving this way and that, lurching and coming to sudden stops, all very different from sluggish London cabs.

I checked the time.

It was already two.

'Is it far?' I asked the driver, but he didn't reply.

I tried again, louder, and this time he heard.

'No, it's not far,' he said.

I turned to Benjamin, and knowing now I had to shout for the driver to hear me, I felt safer talking about money.

'Benjamin,' I said.

'Yes?'

'I need your help.'

'Can Stan help too?'

'Is he good at counting?'

'Very. Ravens are very clever.'

'Good. Because I need to sort our money out. I should have done it on the plane, but . . .'

But there'd been other distractions, on the plane.

I took out the bundle of notes from my bag. I'd taken five hundred dollars from a machine at the airport. It was complicated. I can just about cope with the cashpoint Mum always uses at the end of our street, but they all work slightly differently and this one was able to dispense pounds or euros or dollars. I had to get Benjamin to help me, and at the same time keep him from touching anything himself, just in case he crashed it. There was Braille next to some of the keys, but not all of them. Someone once told me that the toilet doors on trains have the controls marked in Braille, but that was news to me; I've never found them. And there was another thing the cash machine didn't tell you: how the five hundred dollars was broken down.

So in the taxi, I showed it all to Benjamin.

'Here,' I said. 'Are they all worth the same?'

'No, there's different ones.'

'But they're all the same size,' I said. 'Are you sure?'

'I know but there're different numbers on them.'

He grabbed them from me.

'Don't lose any!' I said, at the thought of him dropping them on the floor.

'I won't,' he said, and he sounded a bit cross.

'What have we got?'

'Shh, I'm counting.'

'Benjamin . . . '

'We've got three of these. They're a hundred dollars each.'

'Okay.'

'Then we have three of these. They're fifty each.'

'That's four hundred and fifty so far.'

'And then there are two twenties and one ten.'

'And they're all the same size?'

'Yes, can't you feel?'

154

'Of course I can,' I said. 'It just makes it harder for me.'

'Why?' asked Benjamin, but then he understood. 'Oh, yes. Is our money different sizes?'

'Euros are too,' I said, thinking about the skiing trip. 'Never mind. Give me the hundreds, please.'

He pulled my hand out and pushed the money in. I folded the notes up tightly and put them in the right pocket of my jeans.

'Now the fifties.'

Those went in my left-hand pocket, and then I held the twenties in one hand and the ten in the other until the taxi pulled up.

'Queens Borough Public Library!' announced the driver. 'Twenty-two dollars and eighty cents.'

I held out one of the twenties and the ten and waited with my hand out. The driver gave me some notes and a couple of coins and we scrambled from the taxi, and only as it pulled away did I remember I should have given him a tip.

I didn't know what money he'd given me back, only that it came to seven dollars and twenty cents, but we were late already and I didn't want to waste time working it out, so I shoved it at Benjamin, and put the other twenty in my back pocket.

'Here,' I said. 'Keep this safe for me, please. See anything that looks like a library?'

I felt Benjamin turning round to look.

'Oh, yes,' he said. 'Wow.'

## One Weird Dude

Who knows why people are the way they are? Dad says most people don't even know much about themselves, never mind anyone else. So why Mr Walker was like he was remains a mystery, but I for one came to like it. So who cares?

∽∾┽

'You okay?' I said to Benjamin as we went into the library. He seemed very quiet.

'Mmm,' he said.

'What does that mean?'

'It means I'm tired. You know how you told me the time is different here? So it's already midnight or something . . . ?'

'Benjamin,' I said firmly. 'Even at home it is only seven o'clock in the evening. If I told you to go to bed at seven you'd laugh at me. But here it is two o'clock and that's how we're going to think about it, right?'

I felt exhausted myself. The flight had been tiring, the heat was making it hard to think. I told myself it was only the afternoon and that way I might just get through the day. We were a bit overdressed, though, and I took off my hoodie and made Benjamin take his off too and put them in our bags.

'Okay, Laureth.'

'Okay.'

'But Stan's tired.'

'Well, he can have a nap if he wants but we have to find Mr Walker.'

'How will we find him?'

'He's going to find us.'

'How?'

'I told him what we look like.'

Benjamin stopped walking.

'But this place is enormous. And it's packed.'

I could hear his desperation.

'Can you see a room with lots of people sitting at tables, reading?'

'Yes. It's through those doors.'

'So lead on,' I said, and we were just heading inside when a kid's voice spoke, right next to me.

'Do you know Jack Peak?'

I stopped dead, because no one knew me in New York.

'Who are you?' I asked, turning towards the voice.

'I would have thought that was obvious. Do you know Jack Peak? Did he send you? He must have. You've got the seven-year-old boy and the bird.'

'You . . .' I said. 'You're Mr Walker's son, are you? I'm sorry we're late, we—'

'I'm not Mr Walker's *son*,' he said. 'I'm Mr Walker.'

'Mr Walker? Michael Walker? Oh, I'm sorry, but you sound like a child.'

'I am not a child,' he said. 'I'm twelve. *That's* a child.'

'Hey!' said Benjamin.

I tried not to laugh.

'You called yourself Mr Walker. I'm sorry. I thought you were an adult, that's all.'

'That's merely a name we let society pin upon us, wouldn't you say?'

I didn't know what to say. He might have been twelve but he certainly spoke like an adult. An adult from 1872 to be precise.

'You're the one I was emailing?' I said. 'You found the notebook?'

'I did,' said Mr Walker. 'Pleased to meet you. You may call me Michael.'

I put my hand out as quickly as I could. If you get to the space first it means people have to put their hand where yours already is, not the other way round.

'Laureth. And this is Benjamin.'

'Hello, Benjamin. How'd do you do?'

'And this is Stan,' said Benjamin.

'Good afternoon, Stan,' said Michael, and I started to like him a bit more.

'Do you have the book?'

'I do. Shall we go and find somewhere less public in which to engage in our transaction?'

Then I started to like him a bit less. I didn't want to be led anywhere by a child I'd only just met, especially as I thought I was meeting an adult.

'Listen, Mr Walker. Michael. Where are we going? I just want the notebook and I have the reward money with me, so can we . . . '

'My dear Laureth,' he said. 'Please do not be alarmed. I merely advise you that it is unwise to be seen to display sums of money in such a public area. You act as if you do not trust me.'

'Well, to be fair, you were supposed to be a grown-up, and—'

'Why was I supposed to? You made that assumption. I prefer to call myself Mr Walker to people with whom I have not yet made a formal introduction.'

I was reduced to speechlessness once more.

'You yourself, it appears, are not as old as I was expecting. Nor of the same name. Nor even the same gender.'

'Fair enough,' I said. 'I look after my dad's emails, that's all. I thought I'd get his notebook back for him.'

'Why didn't he come himself? Does he usually send his children around the city to run errands?'

'No, no,' I said. 'It's just that . . . Look. I'm sorry, you're right. Let's go and sit somewhere less noisy.'

So he led us out of the library and back into the

burning heat of the afternoon. I could smell the city wilting; exhaust from cars, even the scent of the tarmac melting under our feet.

He took us down the side of the building and we sat on a bench in the shade but it was still hard to breathe in the humidity.

'I have calculated that fifty British pounds is worth seventy-nine dollars. You can round that up to eighty if you like since I had to come out on such a hot afternoon.'

'I can, can I?' I said. 'Just give me the stupid book and you can have a hundred dollars.'

'A hundred . . . !' began Michael, and for a second I heard that there might be a little kid underneath his posh voice after all. He recomposed himself quickly, though. 'Very well,' he said, 'Here it is.'

I put out my hands but before I could find the book Benjamin took it and placed it there.

'Benjamin?' I said.

'Yes, that's it,' he said.

'Sure?'

'Is there some reason you need your little brother's opinion on this?' asked Michael, back in character.

'Yes, there is,' I said. 'I can't see. I'm blind.'

'Ah,' said Michael. 'Something else you didn't see fit to tell me.'

'I don't see why I should have done.'

'Just as I don't see why it was relevant to mention that I'm a young adult.'

'You've already made your point,' I said. I fished in my right-hand pocket and peeled off one of the hundreds. 'My dad's a generous man. I'm sure he'd be happy for you to have the extra twenty-one.'

'You still haven't told me why he didn't come himself.'

'You're right,' I said. 'I didn't. Anyway, for that extra twenty-one, perhaps you could tell me where you found the notebook?'

'Does it matter?'

'It matters a lot.'

'Why?'

But that's what I didn't want to tell him. I'd only just met him, I didn't trust him. He'd turned out to be some goofy twelve-year-old who spoke as if he had stepped from the pages of Dickens. And I was starting to panic about everything I'd got us into; flying to America without a plan or even a return ticket. What on earth had I been thinking? I knew I'd been angry with Mum but that seemed a pretty pathetic reason right then.

I was worried about Dad too; not just that he'd gone astray, but that something seriously bad had happened to him. How did I know this peculiar child wasn't something to do with it? He had the notebook, after all.

I tried to keep my voice calmer than I felt.

'It matters a lot. Where did you find it?'

'I just found it.'

'So you said in your email. But where?'

Michael sighed.

'It means nothing to me, and probably nothing to you. I was sitting among the trees by the railroad tracks, on the vacant lot on Baisley Boulevard. I like to go there on days when I don't care to visit school. I go there in vacations too. It's quiet and dark and no one . . . Anyway, I was sitting there yesterday morning re-reading *Pride and Prejudice* when out of the sky the book fell on the ground, at my feet. Came down through the trees. I thought it was a bird or something at first. That's all I know. Then I emailed you. And here we are.'

'It fell? From the sky?'

164

'Just as I said.'

I hesitated. That couldn't be all. I had to get him to tell me more, but I couldn't tell him about Dad. Not in front of Benjamin, anyway.

'Benjamin. You still have that money from the taxi?'

'Uh-huh.'

'Yes, Laureth,' I said, bored with myself for sounding so tiresome, but Michael chipped in with 'Quite right!'

'Yes, Laureth.'

'Good. Is there a place on the street selling drinks, in sight of here?'

'Yes. There's a stand over there.'

'Close by?'

'Yes, of course.'

'Good. Go and get us all a drink and buy yourself something to eat if you want. Okay?'

'Okay,' he said, and I handed him the other twenty so he had enough money.

'Why did you do that?' asked Michael when Benjamin had gone.

'Please,' I said. 'Please. Can you keep an eye on him? He's sensible, but . . .'

'Very well,' Michael said.

Then I began to tell him, and once I'd started, I couldn't stop.

'Look. The thing is . . . Our dad's gone missing. I know he's in New York because he must have been here for you to find his book. Mum doesn't care and Benjamin doesn't understand, but I know he's here and I want to find him. I'm really worried but I can't tell Benjamin because I don't want to scare him, so please, please, if you know something else, anything else, then tell me.'

Michael listened to me and then he said, 'I'm very sorry to hear it. I promise you I don't know anything else about it. I'm sorry.'

I felt so tired, and scared, I didn't know what to do next.

'Benjamin's coming back,' Michael said quietly. 'There's one thing, though. As you know I have leafed through the book, primarily to ascertain its contents, but also to photograph certain pages, which I emailed you as verification. There was a bar receipt tucked inside the cover, a receipt from a hotel.'

'A hotel? Do you think it's where he was staying?'

'That we cannot know, but it surely means he

visited there, at least. Perhaps you could go and ask them?'

Benjamin shuffled up.

'Would you like some water, Michael?' he asked, and I was so proud of him for being so polite.

'Thank you, Benjamin.'

I heard him stand.

'Good luck with . . . with everything. The hotel is called The Black King. It's in Manhattan.'

'How do we get there?'

'A taxi will do it. You appear to have enough of those crisp greenbacks. On which note,' he added, 'I'd be a bit more careful how you wave it around.'

'I will,' I said, though I felt stupid, being lectured by a twelve-year-old.

'Good luck. Goodbye, Benjamin, Stan.'

His footsteps were swallowed in the roar of traffic as we approached the street.

'Well,' said Benjamin. 'Are we going to find Dad now?'

'Yes,' I said. 'We are.'

I hoped I sounded more certain than I felt.

'Laureth?'

'What?'

'Mr Walker was one weird dude, wasn't he?'

I laughed.

'Where on earth did you hear an expression like that?'

'The man who sold me the water said it. He asked if we were friends with Michael. He says he's always hanging out around here.'

'Maybe he's no weirder than the rest of us,' I said, and I thought again about what Dad says; who knows why we are the way we are?

So then Benjamin told me when to stick my hand in the air and very soon we were driving into Manhattan in another taxi, heading for The Black King Hotel.

On the way, I got Benjamin to tell me the date and the time on the receipt. It was from Thursday night, around 11p.m. Just two days ago. It was strange, like almost meeting Dad, and then just missing him. So close. So close it felt like I could reach out and touch him. But that wasn't true. He could be anywhere by now, anywhere in the world.

Then I got Benjamin to start reading through Dad's notebook, from the start, looking for anything, *anything*, that might lead us to him.

He started to read, at the beginning, like Dad would have said, and from the very first page there was a lot of talk about one man; a man called Carl Jung.

# TWO CRAZY GUYS

'Knows nothing!'

That's what Freud once said about Jung, apparently, and yet the two men were once firm friends.

\* \* \*

Might be an idea to include some stuff about Jung.

Carl Jung and Sigmund Freud pretty much responsible for the

birth of psychoanalysis. Tour the
US together in 1908 to lecture on the
subject.

Then their friendship dissolves and
Jung develops new ideas, goes off in
a new direction, his work becomes
more mysterious, more mystical,
including not just psychoanalysis but
quantum physics, as well as religion
and mythology. UFOs.

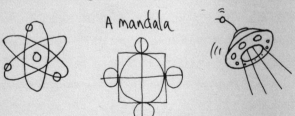

A mandala

In the 20s he develops his ideas
about synchronicity, but doesn't

write about it until the early 1950s,
thirty years later.

Jung is one of the
few thinkers to do serious
work on coincidence, using
statistics to investigate whether
there is any reality behind astrology.
His results were inconclusive, and
remain disputed. Instead he began to
consider coincidence differently.

THERE'S HOPE FOR ME YET!

* * *

He called synchronicity a ' connecting
principle` between people, or objects,
or events, or indeed any combination

of these things. But he said that the connections that occurred during a coincidence were not due to 'cause and effect', but that they were 'acausal', which means that one thing had not CAUSED the other thing to happen. Instead of CAUSALITY therefore, he explained that things could be connected by their MEANING; so the link between seeing a picture of a salmon just as you're talking to a man called Salmon is that they share the same meaning.

Hmm.

Jung first thought about coincidence long before all that. One day he was

treating a female patient who had
dreamed about a scarab beetle, and
just as she was telling him about the
dream, a similar beetle was crawling
over the glass of his office window.
It struck him as very odd indeed, and
so began his lifelong obsession with
coincidence.

He would come to discuss it
with other great men of his age and
he ended up influencing many other
thinkers.

He first discussed it with Albert
Einstein over a series of dinners
between 1909 and 1913 in Zurich.
Einstein famously said: ' God does

not play dice'. By this he meant that the universe has fixed rules and that all you need to do to understand the universe, and everything in it, is discover what these rules are.

Einstein also said this: 'Coincidence is God's way of remaining anonymous.'

What did he mean by that??

Maybe he meant that he didn't believe coincidences had any deep meaning. He was poking fun at people who think they do –

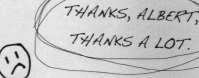
THANKS, ALBERT, THANKS A LOT.

– people who think that coincidences are the clues to some hidden meanings in the universe, some deep knowledge, some great arcane and occult secret.

But is that right?

Can that be right when everything about the feeling of coincidences tells us that THEY MEAN SOMETHING.

We all know they do. We simply feel it.

But what?

What do they mean?

# *The Black King*

That fear had begun to crawl into me was undeniable. I knew I was fighting against it, trying to stop it taking hold. I knew that what I had done was irresponsible. In fact, I knew that what I had done was dangerous, and I wondered how much trouble I would be in. But every time I thought about that I also thought about Dad. I *knew* something was wrong. I'd had no replies to my texts, which was totally unlike him. When I tried to call his phone again from the taxi into Manhattan I got the recorded voice. It was Dad that I was really scared about, and if only I could find him then it wouldn't matter how much trouble I was in.

Benjamin struggled to read Dad's notebook to me, and who can blame him – the notes were strange, very hard to understand. Sometimes there were just lists of words, other times short essays.

Once or twice Benjamin would read something that had nothing to do with *that* book; like a note that Dad had written to remind him to buy me a birthday present. That felt odd. It was like seeing inside Dad's thoughts and it didn't feel right, but it was nice too. It made me think of the last time we'd been together. He'd driven me back to King's College one Sunday night, a few weeks before.

'Going to be gone a while,' he'd said. 'Research trip.'

To be honest, I was worried about some stuff at school. It was the week before our drama assessment, and I hate drama. Standing in front of everyone, trying to pretend to be someone else. I dread it.

I think Dad was saying something about Austria. Or maybe Switzerland. And then we were there and I rushed off before I even heard the car pull away.

When I remembered that I ached inside, and tried to focus on the book instead.

It was so confusing, Benjamin had a tough time of it. I was hoping for a clue of some kind, something that would take us straight to Dad, but all there was so far was rambling passages about Carl Jung, and about what he thought about coincidences.

'Why is Dad so interested in co-inky-dinks?' Benjamin said.

'I don't know,' I said. 'Because he had a big one happen to him, I suppose.'

'Mum says he's obsessed,' Benjamin said.

I didn't reply.

'What does obsessed mean?' Benjamin said.

I opened my mouth, then shut it. Then opened it again and said, 'It's when you like something, a lot.'

Too much, I thought, but kept that to myself.

'Like I like Stan, you mean?'

'No, not quite, more like . . . '

Then Benjamin said, 'Wow,' and had obviously seen something, and I didn't have to explain any further.

'What is it?' I asked.

'We're crossing a huge river. On a big bridge. A big, big bridge. And there are lots of skyscrapers. It's just like in *Godzilla*.'

'Oh,' I said, 'that must be Manhattan. We'll be at the hotel soon. Listen, Benjamin, can you read me a couple more pages?'

'They're boring, Laureth. I don't want to. I want to look at the buildings.'

'I know, but it's important. We—'

I stopped. Benjamin needed a break. To be honest, so did I. I was tired, and Dad's notebook was doing my head in. Something about it scared me. Parts seemed coherent, but other bits were peculiar and disjointed, and it worried me that the Black Book was a reflection of Dad's *state of mind*. But then, I'd never known how his notebooks work. He'd never read them to me before; I don't even think he let Mum look inside them. Not that she was interested, not anymore. Maybe they were always like this; fragmented and odd.

Dad's always talking about writers. How they hear characters speaking to them and are compelled to write about them. He says if other people hear voices in their heads they get locked up in rooms that have nothing sharp in them. Maybe writers are just a bit bonkers anyway. Maybe any writer's Google searches would get a normal person committed.

The taxi was stopping and starting in Saturday afternoon traffic. There were the sounds of horns, of cars and bigger vehicles, and I could tell the city was busy.

'What do you see?' I asked Benjamin.

'Wow,' he said.

I was glad Benjamin was happy. He still didn't seem to understand that we were doing something very unusual, but he's not stupid, and I wondered how long it would be before he figured out I really didn't have a clue where Dad was. Then he might get upset, and scared, and I couldn't afford for that to happen. I couldn't do this without him, so he had to stay happy. A wave of tiredness came over me, but I pushed it away, and from nowhere a new thought occurred to me, one that frightened me more than anything.

Maybe Dad didn't want to be found. Maybe he had left Mum. Maybe he had left her and just not *told* her yet. Maybe he *had* told her, and she was just not telling us; Benjamin and me. I knew things were bad between them but somehow I'd never imagined they'd split up, perhaps because I'd never allowed that thought to enter my head.

What had Mum said?

*Right now, I could not possibly care less where your father is.*

I went cold. Just like that, it hit me. They had broken up, and not told me, and then I felt a lot of things at once; fear, and anger, and I wanted to cry, but I couldn't, because there was Benjamin to think of. I had to hold it together, but then the taxi came to another stop, and this time the driver mumbled something.

'Pardon?' I called.

'Thirty-five dollars and forty cents.'

I wasn't ready with the money.

'Benjamin,' I said. 'What do you have?'

Between us we fished around and found the right money plus a little tip.

'Which side is the kerb?' I asked Benjamin.

'Your side.'

'Well, scoot over here and come out with me.'

We got out.

'Can you see the hotel? It's called the . . . '

'The Black King,' said Benjamin. 'I know. There's a huge picture of a playing card by the door. The King of Spades.'

Benjamin was holding my hand and began to tug. I pulled him back.

'Listen, Benjamin. I want you to let me do the talking in there, okay?'

'Why, Laureth?'

'I just do. But I want you to do your best job ever of guiding me. Please. We need to find the reception desk.'

'Laureth, it's hot.'

'I know. It will be cooler inside. They'll have air-conditioning. Come on. Do you have Stan?'

'Yes.'

We went inside and my heart was already pounding, because this was our only lead, and if it turned out that Dad wasn't here, I would sit down and cry.

My throat felt dry despite drinking the whole bottle of water Benjamin had bought me, and another blast of tiredness came and went. We pushed through the doors, which decided to leap out and bump me on the shoulder, and then we were greeted by a wall of noise, and an icy blast of air-conditioning.

The sound of people talking was almost overwhelming.

'Where are we?' I shouted to Benjamin, and even then he only just heard me.

'It's like a coffee shop, or a bar, or something. There's *thousands* of people.'

I guessed he might be exaggerating a bit, but maybe not by much.

'Are you're sure we're in the hotel?'

'Yes.'

'Can you see the reception desk?'

'Yes, over here,' he said. 'I think.'

'You think?'

'I'm doing my best,' he said. 'It's hard to tell. It's really dark in here.'

Even I could tell that.

Benjamin began to steer me over to the desk. He pulled me to a stop.

'Queue,' he said.

We waited a minute and I listened to the sprawl of chatter and laughter from the lobby. There was loud music playing, something with a weird beat that seemed to stop, fall over itself, and then start again.

Benjamin squeezed my hand, and took me up to the desk.

A young man's voice greeted us.

'Hi. I'm Brett. How may I help you?'

He sounded friendly, but I felt nervous. What would happen if Dad wasn't here? What would happen if he was?

'Er, yes, hello,' I said. 'I believe you have Mr Peak staying here? Jack Peak?'

It can only have been a moment's pause in which Brett didn't reply, but it felt like eternity.

Please, I thought. Please. Please let him be here.

'Well, yes, we do.'

I couldn't help but smile.

'Yes, good,' I said. 'Good.'

I squeezed Benjamin's hand.

'Dad's here?' Benjamin said.

'Shh!' I said, quickly. 'You know he is. Remember what I told you.'

'Miss?'

It was Brett, behind the desk.

There was a little hesitation in his voice, and I realised that hotels have rules on giving out information about their guests.

'Oh, it's okay. He's our father. We've come to join him. He's been here and we've come to join him.'

'We have no record of other guests on the reservation,' said Brett.

'Oh, well that's Dad for you,' I said. 'He'll have forgotten to tell you. We only came into town today. To meet him. We've been . . . upstate.'

I don't know why I said that. But I did and it sounded plausible, and that made me feel in control.

'We've been what?' asked Benjamin, and I squeezed his hand so hard I think I might have hurt him, but he was quiet.

'Mr Peak isn't in right now,' said Brett.

'But he told us to meet him here this afternoon. So could we have a key please? And then we can go and wait.'

There was another pause.

'Can I see some ID, please?'

Brett's voice was slightly less friendly.

I showed him our passports and he warmed up again.

'That's great,' he said. I didn't see what was so great, but Brett wasn't done.

'I love your father's books,' he said. 'Those funny ones, the ones he used to write?'

'Uh-huh,' I said. 'So could we have a key, please?'

'Yes, of course,' said Brett. 'Just one thing. For security. You presumably know which room your father is in? He'll have told you that.'

We were so close. I didn't know what to say.

'I'm sorry to ask,' Brett went on. 'But we've had some . . . That is, the hotel manager has told us to be extra careful about security just now. Of course if you don't know the number you could always phone your father and . . . '

'His phone's not working,' I said, 'and we don't know the room number, but please . . . '

'Yes, we do,' said Benjamin. 'We do know the number.'

'Benjamin . . . ' I said, warningly.

'We do know the number. You must have forgotten. It's 354.'

'Benjamin . . . '

'That's the one,' said Brett brightly, and seconds later I heard a piece of plastic clipping down on the metal reception desk.

I stood dumbfounded at what had just happened.

'You're all set,' said Brett. 'Have a good day. The elevators are right behind you. Third floor.'

I fumbled for the card and Benjamin got us in the lift before anyone tried to stop us.

'How did you know that?' I asked as the doors closed on the noise of the lobby.

'Because that's Dad's number, isn't it? The co-inky-dink number.'

'Yes,' I said, 'but that doesn't mean he's staying in that room.'

'Yes it does,' said Benjamin. 'He told me. He always asks for that room when he stays in a hotel. If they have a room 354, I mean.'

'Benjamin,' I laughed, 'you are a totally excellent person.'

He hugged me, and the lift doors pinged open.

'Wow,' said Benjamin. 'It's even darker up here.'

Benjamin pulled my hand, and we stepped onto quiet hotel corridor carpets, looking for room 354.

354, which is, as Benjamin so rightly said, Dad's coincidence number.

I mean, co-inky-dink.

I was so happy.

Dad was here. He was staying in the hotel. Even if he was out right then, we were almost there; we'd found him.

## *354*

It's a pretty weird number to choose if you're setting out to choose a lucky number, but Dad says that's not what it is.

For ages, he's had this thing about the number 354. He says he first started spotting this number years ago, when he was a teenager, that he sees it again and again, so often that he decided it had to mean something.

He calls it *his* number, or sometimes just *the* number. As if there are no other numbers in the world, which is obviously far from the case. There are an infinite number of numbers, or so our maths teacher would have us believe.

A while back, Dad decided to record every instance he comes across of this number. It was on his first trip to New York as a published writer when he started thinking about it again. He was up for some book award, and there was a big dinner happening in Manhattan. His publisher sent a limo to collect him from the airport, and it had a three digit number on it: 354.

He checked in at his hotel, a hotel his publisher had booked for him, and the girl behind the desk handed him his key, yes, that's right: 354.

Since then, as we found out in the Black Book, he's recorded every single time he's seen it since; it goes on for four closely written pages, according to Benjamin. It's as if he's collecting them. Like, I suppose I have to say it, he's obsessed.

It's appeared in phone numbers, on lockers, in limited-edition prints, as page counts in books, as flight numbers, as the price of things, as house numbers and software versions. In short; it's appeared in every single way a number can appear, frequently more than once.

Dad believes this number appears more than any other number, and he also believes it means something.

I told him he only *thinks* he comes across it more often because he's looking for it. And that if he concentrated on some other number, he'd see that one more often instead.

'I know what you're saying,' he said. 'Every day, you're bombarded by numbers, usually long strings of phone numbers. And yes, you're right, occasionally I see 354 in the middle of those numbers and they're the ones I focus on. But tell me why it is I see this number all the time when there are only 3 digits in question? The chances of seeing 354 when given a three-digit number should be about one in 899, right? In 899 times, every number from 100 to 999 should come up once. Yes?'

'I promise you,' he said. 'I see 354 way more than once every 899 times.'

I thought I had him then.

'Ah, yes,' I said. 'If there was an equal chance of each number coming up. But there isn't.'

'No?'

'No. Like the lockers at the swimming pool. I always

195

go for the one on the end if I can so I know where my stuff is. But Benjamin goes for the highest number there is, but that's only two hundred and something.'

Dad was thinking, I could tell.

'You might have something there. When I stayed in room 354 in New York that time for the award . . . The hotel only had five floors of rooms, so the highest number it had would have been 599.'

'Exactly. Sequences of numbers always start at one, don't they? So there must be more instances of lower numbers in the world than high ones.'

'Laureth,' he said, 'you might be right about that. But I still think my number comes up more than it should. Be that as it may, I'm going to investigate what you said.'

If he says he'll do something, he does. Usually.

So off he went and spoke to an old friend of his who is a professor of maths, and he told him two things, which Dad wrote down in his notebook. I know that because it was one of the pages that Michael Walker had mailed back, that Benjamin had read at the airport.

∽∾

First, he told Dad I was right. I was rather pleased with myself about that, but then this guy told Dad there was something really weird about numbers, a thing called Benford's Law.

Benford's Law: what this says is truly strange.

Suppose you have a large set of numbers, such as the amounts of a thousand electricity bills, or the lengths of the rivers of South America, or death rates in Asia, or stock prices, or population numbers.

You might think that there would be the same chance that any of these numbers started with a one, as with a nine. Or any other number for that matter. After all, any number in your set can start with any one of the nine digits, so they ought to all have the same chance of being the first one, right?

Well, apparently not. _Apparently_ 1 will be the first digit of the number 30% of the time, whereas 9 will be the first digit only 5% of the time. And in the middle of these two, the numbers 2 to 8 appear with a precisely measurable decreasing frequency, so 2 appears about 17% of the time, 3 about 12% and so on down to poor old 9 with that measly 5%.

Strange.

* * *

Ah! You say.

Ah! I have an idea! It's to do with the units involved; it biases things towards the lower numbers in some way.

* * *

But here's the really weird thing: change the units you're measuring those rivers in from miles to kilometres, and the effect is the same. Change death rates from per year to per month, and the result is the same. It doesn't matter. The universe simply favours the lower numbers in some way. There are a few explanations of why Benford's Law is true, but not everyone agrees; it's a bit of a mystery.

Benford's Law is so little known, and so misunderstood, that it's even been used in court cases to catch people guilty of fraud. For example, they're making up some numbers to put in their company accounts, and they think they'll look more random if they're evenly spread out across all the nine digits that a number can start with. But they're wrong, and clever lawyers have got people sent to jail as a result.

When Dad told me all this, I didn't understand it at first. But I wanted to, so I got him to tell me over and over again, until I did. And when Benjamin read it, he didn't get it either, but I wasn't as good at explaining it to him as Dad had been to me, so I don't think he got it even when I tried.

But that didn't matter. It didn't matter if it meant anything to Benjamin, or to me, because I could tell it meant something to Dad. He was trying to show me that there are hidden patterns in the universe, that maybe there are some secrets still to be found. Secrets that lie inside the numbers that the universe is built on.

And that maybe the number 354 is one of them.

## *The Empty Room*

Never in my life had I felt so tired, and so excited at the same time. Maybe I was being foolish, but to me it seemed we'd done it. We'd found Dad, or as good as, and I was just desperate to see him and for everything to be okay.

'Can you see 354?' I asked Benjamin as we stepped out of the lift.

'It's hard,' he said. 'The corridor is so dark. There's no lights.'

'There must be some.'

'Well, hardly any.'

'There'll be a sign showing which way to go.'

'I know, Laureth,' he said. 'I'm not stupid. But it's really dark. This hotel is what Dad would call too cool for school.'

'What do you mean?'

'I don't know. But he'd say that, I know he would.'

He pulled my hand and we set off down the length of the corridor.

'This is stupid!' he said, grumbling all the way. 'It's so dark. Anyway, we're here.'

Benjamin showed me where to put the plastic key card that opened room 354. We had to try it about four different ways before it worked, until finally it made an annoying little click, and we let ourselves in.

'Well?' I said, and shut the door behind us.

'What?'

'Is his stuff here?'

'Yes,' said Benjamin. 'His bag's on the table, and his laptop's on the desk. And there's a bunch of jumpers hanging on a rail.'

I thought about the heat outside.

'It's Dad all right. Always packing the wrong clothes.'

'Wow!' said Benjamin. 'It's big. There's another room through a door. Where the bed is.'

I thought about Mum and Dad. I thought about Mum telling Dad he spends too much money, and here he was, paying for a suite in a hotel, in New York. It can't have been cheap.

'So do we meet Dad here?' asked Benjamin.

'I guess so,' I said.

There seemed nothing else to do. His phone wasn't working; there was no way of reaching him. But he had to come back sooner or later.

And we were tired.

We sat on the bed for a bit. Then we both needed the loo, so I went, and then Benjamin did, and while he was in the bathroom, I found Dad's jumpers on the rail. I held onto one of the sleeves, for a long time, as if I was trying to prove to myself that Dad still existed. I lifted the sleeve and touched my cheek with it, trying to will him to walk through the door. He didn't.

Benjamin flushed the loo and I dropped the sleeve.

We sat on the bed again. It was cool in the room; there was an air-conditioning unit under the window, which made a loud hum all the time, but it was good to have.

From outside there was the rumble and honk of traffic; horns and cries from the street below.

We fell asleep, lists of 354s in our heads, but I don't remember anything after that, as if the numbers had hypnotised us.

෨෴

I woke up to the sound of someone knocking on the door.

I pulled my arm out from underneath Benjamin, who had turned into a dead weight.

'Coming!' I said, and though I'd not really been there for long enough to memorise it fully, I managed to get from the bedroom through the other room and to the door by following the sound of the knocking. I had no idea how long we'd been asleep. It felt like days.

I checked my phone. It had only been fifteen minutes.

'Yes,' I said, opening the door.

'Ah, Miss Peak? May I come in?'

It was a woman's voice.

I'd forgotten to put my sunglasses on. She'd see I was blind, but I supposed that didn't matter anymore.

'I'm Margery Lundberg,' said the woman, in a voice that can only be described as smooth. So I wasn't surprised when she added, 'I'm the hotel manager.'

'Er, yes,' I said, already panicking. 'Come in.'

I let her step inside, and shut the door behind her.

'Just a minute,' I said. 'My brother's asleep. He's tired out.'

I was tired out too, but I didn't want to show it. I found my way to the bedroom door, and tried to close it. I couldn't. For some reason it wouldn't move.

'Here, let me help you with that,' said Margery Lundberg. 'It's a sliding door.'

I felt her brush past me and heard her slide the door closed, easily.

'Is something wrong?' I said.

Of course something was wrong. Why else would she be here?

'No,' she said, in that way that means yes. 'No, only I understand from Brett on the front desk that you've joined your father at our hotel.'

'Yes,' I said, as breezily as I could manage. 'We've just got here.'

'Brett mentioned that you are . . . sixteen, Miss?'

'I am.'

'And is your mother here too?'

'Oh, yes, she's on her way. Maybe later, I think.'

'You think?'

'Yes. Is there something wrong, Mrs Lundberg?'

'Margery, please,' she said. Smoothly. 'It's just that we have a policy about minors staying alone in the hotel.'

'Minors? Oh, you mean . . . But we're not alone. Dad's here.'

'Your father checked in to the hotel yesterday, but he did not sleep here. Last night.'

'I'm sorry, I—'

'So I wonder if we should check that your father is coming back tonight. Because we have a policy about minors staying alone.'

'Yes,' I said, and I thought, and I'll bet it's not a policy I want to hear right now.

'Yes?'

'Oh, yes,' I said. 'He's back later. We're meeting up. Later on.'

'Okay then,' said Margery, in that way people do when they have nothing further to say, though they'd really like to. 'Okay.'

'Good,' I said. 'Thanks for checking, though. Thanks.'

And I managed to get rid of her.

'Okay,' she said, as I shut the door on her.

I slid the door open and hurried into the bedroom, and though I hated doing it, I shook Benjamin awake.

'Escalator mice!' he cried, or something similar, and I wondered what kind of weird dream he'd been having. I shook him some more.

'What, Laureth? What? I want to sleep.'

'I know you do,' I said. 'But you can't. We have to find Dad.'

'But Dad's coming here. You said—'

'He might be. But we have to find him before tonight. They don't want us in here by ourselves. This woman called Margery just came and told me. We have to find Dad now.'

Benjamin moaned, but I pulled him upright. He yawned.

'Okay,' he said. 'How?'

'I don't know,' I said. 'Maybe there's something

209

in the room that will tell us where he's gone. Or something in the notebook.'

'Like a clue?' said Benjamin, sounding more awake.

'Yes,' I said. 'Just like a clue. Find the last page he wrote in - that will be what he wrote about most recently. See what it says.'

Benjamin found the Black Book and began to flick through the pages.

As he did, I thought about Margery Lundberg. She'd been pretty abrupt with me. I could tell she didn't like me. But she hadn't treated me as if I was stupid, because I hadn't allowed her to. That's one of the things about being blind; you have to be confident, or people think you're stupid, and treat you that way. And if you don't feel confident, you have to pretend you are. That's just how it is.

But it felt hopeless. I was letting Benjamin get carried away, looking for clues in the Black Book as if he was actually going to find something, when all that was going to happen was that he'd find nothing, and we'd get thrown out of the hotel.

So I was feeling pretty much desperate, and then Benjamin said, 'I've found something.'

'What?'

'I've found the last page he's written in,' he said.

'Read it,' I said, desperate for anything that might help us.

'Edgar Allan Poe Cottage. 2640 Grand Concourse. The Bronx. Open Saturday ten a.m. to four p.m. Appt with Valerie Braun, three p.m. What's "Appt"?'

'That's it!' I cried. 'That's it. "Appt" means appointment. Three p.m.? He's probably there now. Come on!'

I checked my phone. It was half past three.

I had no idea where this place was, but Dad had an appointment there. That had to be it. If we hurried, we might find him, and if we didn't, and he decided to spend another night away from his hotel room for some unknown reason, I didn't like to think what Margery Lundberg would have to say about that.

I emptied my bag of everything but my phone and the notebook, and Benjamin left everything. Everything apart from Stan of course, and we headed back outside to find a taxi.

The lift seemed to have given up, and after waiting a few minutes we gave up too.

'Are there any stairs?'

'Yes,' said Benjamin. 'There. Be careful though, it's tricky.'

What he meant, as I found out by stumbling, was that the first step down was actually in the corridor, not in the stairwell itself.

'Thanks,' I said. I used to hate stairs, but they're one of those things you have to tackle in life, like kettles. I was scared of them for a long time too; nasty hissing, boiling monsters. In the end, you just have to say; I'm going to beat that thing. It will submit to me. And in that way, you get there, you win. You have to pretend you're not scared, even when you are.

The lobby was just as loud as it was before, and on top of that, as we made our way out there seemed to be an argument going on. There was a strong smell of stale smoke and I could hear Margery Lundberg and Brett, as well as someone else's voice, all mixed in the noise of the entrance.

'Please understand,' Margery was saying. 'We've already asked you to leave, and I am not afraid to call the police to deal with this matter.'

She was clearly not someone to mess about with, and I began to pray Dad was still at his meeting. We hurried by, glad she had something to occupy her other than unaccompanied minors staying in her hotel.

The bellhop at the door found a taxi for us, and we crawled off into the New York traffic.

# The Dying Poet

'Been thinking,' said Benjamin.

'Benjamin,' I said. 'I know you're tired, but you ought to say "I've".'

'I've been thinking,' he said, and I hated myself a bit for being so picky with him. Things were bad enough for Benjamin as it was, he didn't need his big sister giving him a hard time too.

'What have you been thinking?' I asked.

'I was thinking about Dad.'

'Oh,' I said, because so had I.

'Is he really here somewhere?'

'Of course he is!' I said. 'You just saw his stuff, didn't you?'

So then Benjamin was silent but I wondered why I didn't feel reassured by what I'd just said. I was thinking about Dad too, and about Mum. And about love.

Love is a funny thing, and once again I really don't mean it's amusing. I mean it's odd. Strange. Weird.

There was a time not so long ago, because I can remember it, when Mum and Dad loved each other. It was obvious, in the things that they did, and the way they were, and the way they called each other 'honey'.

But I no longer believed that they did. It was obvious, in the things that they did, and the way that they were. And the way they called each other 'honey'. In just the wrong tone of voice, through teeth held tight.

I wondered why Dad had checked into a hotel, and then not slept there, and when I thought about the possible reasons, the very *best* one was that he was sleeping with someone else. And the worst, I liked even less, because that was that something *really* bad had happened. And since, even if he *was* having some kind of affair, he'd have still answered my texts, the worse option looked the most likely. I started to feel sick about what that might be.

In the taxi, I thought about phoning Mum.

Or at least, texting her.

She'd be at Auntie Sarah's. At the party. I noted that she hadn't texted Benjamin and me, to see if we were okay, but decided not to worry about that, because I had enough to worry about already. Suddenly I wondered whether my phone even worked in America. Maybe Mum wasn't paying for that kind of contract. I realised I had absolutely no idea.

I took my phone out, and fiddled with it a bit, then put it away. But I told myself that if it got to evening and we still hadn't found Dad, I'd text her, or try to, at least. I'd text her and tell the truth.

I asked the taxi driver how long it would take to get to 2640 Grand Concourse, the Bronx, and he told me the traffic wasn't his fault.

I told him I didn't think it was and he told me it could be ten minutes or it could be an hour.

On the way, we went through the most recent pages of Dad's book, in detail, slowly, and it turned out they were about another writer; a long dead American called

Edgar Allan Poe. I knew a few bits of his writing from English lessons, when we'd studied Gothic fiction. The best thing was a long poem called 'The Raven', and not just because it reminded me of Stan. It was kind of over-the-top, but I liked it a lot. Anyway, Dad's entry in his notebook wasn't about Poe's writing, but his life.

It started with a list of the most famous and most outrageously unbelievable coincidences of all time.

There were stories about babies falling out of windows and landing on their long-lost father walking underneath. Stories about lost objects turning up years later in unlikely places (like Dad's Jung book) and a whole page of coincidences that connected the assassinations of two American presidents, Lincoln and Kennedy, a hundred years apart.

But the next page was given over to what Dad thinks is the best coincidence of all time – that of Edgar Allan Poe and Richard Parker. He's told me it before, so I wasn't surprised, but I wanted Benjamin to read the page anyway, in case there was something else that could help us.

In 1838 Edgar Allan Poe wrote his only full-length novel; _The Narrative of Arthur Gordon Pym of Nantucket_, a fantastical tale about a young man who stows away on a whaling ship and embarks on wild adventures. In one section of the book, the ship sinks and there are only four survivors; one of them, called Richard Parker, suggests that they should draw lots, the loser to be eaten by the others. They do so, and Parker loses, and is cannibalised by his shipmates.

So much for fiction.

Back in the real world, in 1884, a yacht known as the Mignonette sank. Only four of the crew survived; three hands and the cabin boy. He was killed and eaten by his shipmates. His name was Richard Parker.

I could just hear Dad saying 'fact is stranger than fiction'. He says authors like to say that a lot. Usually, he says, when they've written a bit of their book that's so unbelievable it stinks.

I could also hear Dad saying 'life imitates art' and if that's true, then Mr Poe really would have been amazed by what happened in 1884, 35 years after he'd died, when a part of his book came to life.

I felt a bit bad getting Benjamin to read that stuff out, but I know there's far more lurid stuff in his comics. He seemed to like the story about Richard Parker, anyway.

'That's really weird,' he said.

'I know. Dad says it's not the absolute weirdest coincidence. But he thinks it's the best because there's no way it could be made up. Poe wrote that book. And that ship really sank.'

'No one made that bit up?'

'No. It was a famous case. The survivors were taken to court. You can read old newspapers about it. You can see Richard Parker's grave. Dad's been there.'

'His *grave*?' asked Benjamin. I could tell his mind was working. 'What's inside it?'

'Never mind,' I said. Though I had to admit, he had a point.

'Where are we going anyway?' Benjamin asked, as the taxi suddenly surged ahead and then slowed to crawl again through traffic.

'I think it's a museum,' I said. 'Where Edgar Allan Poe lived. Dad is meeting someone there. I think he probably wants to talk about Poe.'

I told Benjamin some of the things Mr Woodell had told us about him in English, the main one being that he died in mysterious circumstances, like something out of one of his own stories.

Poe went missing, and although he was found after about a week, he was in great distress, delirious, and never fully regained consciousness. He was found wearing someone else's clothes, and kept calling out the name Reynolds. No one knew who that was. After four days, he died, and the mystery of his death has never been solved.

I could think of another writer who had gone missing.

Another coincidence? Life imitating *life*, this time?

If that were true, I needed the coincidences to stop before it got to an ending I did not like.

# The Poet's Home

'Her idea of a good time,' I heard Benjamin whispering to Stan. 'Driving all over New York.'

'What did you say?' I asked, though I didn't really have the heart to be cross.

'It's rude to listen to other people's conversations.'

'Well, it's rude to speak about people like that too,' I snapped.

I was tired. I was really tired, and I was grumpy like you get when you're that exhausted. Our taxi, which had been stopping and starting with the rest of the traffic, suddenly sped up, and kept going. We must have reached a different part of town. I tried to calm down a bit and remember that Benjamin was only seven.

'Where are we?' I asked him.

'I don't know.'

'What can you see?'

'Nothing,' said Benjamin.

'What?'

'I can't see anything. It's all black. Stan's sitting on my face.'

I counted to five and then I asked Benjamin if he could ask Stan to stop sitting on Benjamin's face and help look out of the window.

'Wow!' said Benjamin. 'Hey! Can we stop?'

'No we can't. Why?'

'There was an awesome comic shop! We just passed it. Can we stop and have a look?'

'No, Benjamin, we can't. I'm sorry.'

'But it was so cool. Please?'

'We'll see. Find out what street we're on and we can come back.'

'Oh, Laureth . . . '

'Benjamin. We have to go to the museum now.'

'Is Dad there?'

'We'll see.'

'You sound like Mum,' he said. '"We'll see." We *never* see.'

'I'm sorry. We'll come back. I promise. What was the shop called?'

'I didn't see. But we're on a street called Broadway.'

'How can you be sure?'

'Easy,' said Benjamin. 'There's a map of where we are on the TV.'

'A what?'

'There's a little TV in every taxi we've been in. This one has a map of where we are, like satnav.'

So that was what I thought had been the radio; there was the same perpetual chatter of a news channel coming from it.

'You can see where we are?'

'Yes,' said Benjamin. He was silent for ages. And then he said, 'New York.'

'Very funny.'

'It was Stan's joke.'

'Is that right?'

'Yes,' said Benjamin. 'That's right.'

I smiled.

'It was a very funny joke,' I said, thinking about

the screen and what had happened at Border Control at JFK.

'Don't touch it,' I warned him.

'I'm not going to!' he said, but something about the way he said it told me his hand was halfway towards it. He slumped back into the seat next to me.

There was silence, and then the muffled voice of Benjamin saying, 'Stan's sitting on my face again.'

'Stan,' I said, tired, 'stop it.'

Now the taxi was finally moving fast I felt better than when we'd been crawling through traffic. We drove for another ten minutes or so, and then eventually, we came to a standstill.

I paid the driver, and just as we were getting out, he said, 'You know where you're going, Miss?'

'Yes,' I said.

'You take good care of yourself,' he said.

'I will.'

I hesitated.

'Er, excuse me, we're looking for the Edgar Allan Poe Cottage. Is it here?'

'Ain't nothing here,' said the driver, ''cepting the Grand Concourse. Which ain't so grand anymore. Unless and except it's that little white building in the park, over there.'

'Benjamin?'

'I see it, Laureth.'

That had to be it. I thanked the driver and we headed towards the park, Benjamin, Stan, and me.

I checked my phone.

It was 3:54.

I told myself that was a positive omen.

'Can you see a way in?'

Benjamin thought for a minute.

'Yes, I think it's down here. There's railings. Laureth, it's tiny. Are you sure Dad's here? I can't see him.'

He was holding my hand very tightly.

'Let's find out,' I said.

There were stairs up to the cottage, which I had a little trouble with because Benjamin was pulling ahead to the door, not telling me how many steps there were.

We pushed in through the door, and a woman's voice said, 'I'm sorry. We're about to close.'

I could tell we were standing in a very small room, an entrance hall or something, because the sound was close and flat.

'I know,' I said. 'We know. We came to meet someone.'

'Oh,' said the woman. 'The last visitors just left. We're about to close. But we're open tomorrow from ...'

'I'm sorry,' I said. 'We're looking for our father. He was here at three o'clock. He came here to meet a woman called Valerie Braun.'

'That's me,' said the woman. 'You're Mr Peak's children?'

'Yes. Did you see him? When did he leave?'

'I didn't see him,' Valerie said. 'Your father didn't show up.'

'No,' I said, desperately. 'No, he must have ...'

'I assure you,' said Valerie, 'I have been here all afternoon, and he didn't come. He had an appointment at three, just as you said, but he didn't show. Are you all right?'

I wasn't. I wasn't all right, but I could feel Benjamin starting to get upset, just from the way he held my hand, just from the way he was pulling.

'Yes. We're just trying to find him, and—'

'Are you lost?' Valerie said. She sounded concerned, and I felt tears start to come behind my sunglasses.

'No,' I said, quietly. I wanted to tell her that I

thought it was Dad who was lost, not us. But I daren't do that in front of Benjamin.

'Who are you?' I asked. 'I mean, do you know why Dad wanted to meet you?'

'I'm one of the curators here at the cottage,' said Valerie. 'Your father wanted to speak to an expert on the life of Poe and made an appointment with me.'

'Do you know why?'

'I'm sorry, I don't. He only said he wanted to ask someone about Poe's time in New York. This cottage you're standing in is where Poe lived from 1846 to 1849, the last years of his life.'

I could sense we were in danger of putting Valerie Braun into guided-tour mode, but something she said was odd.

'I thought Poe died somewhere else. Didn't he? I can't remember where.'

'Yes, that's right. He died in Baltimore, but he was only visiting there at the time. This cottage was where he was living up to his death.'

'Oh,' I said. 'Listen, do you think I could ask you something?'

'Yes, Miss?'

'Laureth. My name's Laureth. This is Benjamin.'

'Hello,' said Benjamin. 'And this is Stan.'

Valerie laughed.

'What a nice blackbird,' she said.

Before Benjamin, or Stan, could object to that, I asked Valerie a favour.

'If Dad shows up, could you get him to ring me? Could you tell him we're at the hotel. And we're waiting for him? Could you do that? Please?'

'Are you in some kind of trouble?' asked Valerie, her voice soft and kind.

'No,' I said. 'No, nothing like that. We're fine. Aren't we, Benjamin?'

'Yes, Laureth. But Stan says he's hot.'

'That's that fur coat he's wearing,' said Valerie, laughing at her own joke.

When we didn't join in, she said, 'Yes. I'll get your dad to call you. Maybe he got the day wrong. We're open tomorrow too, from—'

'Yes,' I said. 'Thank you. Thank you very much. Come on, Benjamin.'

I hesitated.

'Just one other thing,' I said to Valerie. 'Did Edgar Allan Poe ever write about coincidences?'

'Coincidences?' she said slowly. 'Not that I can

think of. Of course there is the famous Richard Parker story. You might like to hear—'

'Thank you,' I said, quickly, trying not to sound rude. 'We know that one.'

We left the little museum, and I could feel panic rising in my stomach and my chest.

'Is there somewhere to sit down?' I asked Benjamin.

'What are we going to do now?' he asked.

'We're going to sit down. I want . . .' I tried to keep calm. 'I need to sit down, Benjamin. I just need to think for a minute. Is there somewhere to sit down? In the shade?'

'There's a bench under a tree over there.'

'Is it away from the cottage?'

I didn't want Valerie to leave work and see us. She'd start thinking we were lost again, with nowhere to go and without a clue. She'd have been right.

'What are we going to do now?' Benjamin asked again, as we sat down.

'Do you have any of your water left?'

'No,' he said. 'I'm hungry, too. And Stan says he's starving.'

'We'll get something to eat. And a drink.'

'Laureth,' said Benjamin. 'You don't know where Dad is, do you?'

'Yes, I do. He's . . . We're going to see him later, at the hotel. He—'

'Laureth!' Benjamin said. I could hear that he was crying. 'You don't know where he is. He's gone missing, hasn't he?'

'No, no,' I said. 'He's just . . .'

I put my arms around Benjamin and held him while he cried.

'You don't know where he is,' he wailed.

'I *do*. Well, we know he's at the hotel. He'll be back later and I'm sure we'll see him. Everything's fine. We should have waited there for him. I don't know what came over me.'

'Laureth, I don't believe you!' Benjamin said. 'I'm not stupid. I know you've been pretending this is a game, but it's not! Dad's missing and you don't know how to find him. I want Mummy, I want Mum! I want Mum.'

I held him for a long time. I didn't like to think about Mum, because I didn't like to think about how she didn't seem to care that Dad was missing. If I thought about that, I felt too much on my own, so much it terrified me.

'I'm sorry, Benjamin,' I said quietly. 'I shouldn't have brought you. But I couldn't have done this by myself. You know I couldn't. I just wanted to find Dad. I was silly. I shouldn't have done it.'

He seemed to calm down, and I knew I should have told him the truth from the start. Even though he's small, I should have asked him what he thought, and what he wanted to do, not played this dangerous game.

I held Benjamin until he stopped sobbing, and I told myself I wasn't alone. We weren't alone. I told myself that again and again. I had Benjamin with me, and Stan. We'd find Dad. We had to.

'I'm scared, Laureth,' Benjamin said. 'I'm scared. I want Mum. Aren't you scared?'

And then, that was it, I was crying too.

Because, yes, I was. I am scared, almost all the time. But I never tell anyone. I can't afford to. I have to go on pretending I'm this confident person, because if I don't, if I'm quiet, I become invisible. People treat me as if I'm not there. I remember being tiny, about Benjamin's age, standing in the sweet shop, and the woman behind the counter asking Mum, 'What does she want? Does she like chocolates? Or something else? How do you manage with her? It must be very hard . . .'

She kept on and on, as if I wasn't there. As if I were invisible. But I'm not.

The woman kept on and on, and Mum didn't know what to say, and I just stood there, feeling more and more upset, and as she went on, I suddenly thought it was as if *she* was the one who was blind, and couldn't see me, not the other way around.

So then I learned to speak up for myself. I learned to turn my head towards whoever is speaking; I learned to hold my hand out to greet people. I learned not to rock when I was nervous, or to touch my eyes, and I learned to do a thousand things to help sighted people simply talk to me. I made myself seem how I seem now; confident, outgoing, probably a bit cocky.

People think I have so much faith in myself, but I have none. I have no faith in myself, or in what I can do, and yet people think I can do anything I want.

That's how I seem, but it's an illusion. It's an act, nothing more.

ᕫᔑᒣ

When we'd finished crying, I sat back, but kept hold of Benjamin's hand.

'Listen, Benjamin. I've got it wrong. I did a stupid thing. And if you want, we'll go right back to the airport now and fly home to Mum.'

Benjamin nearly knocked me off the bench as he threw his arms around me again. He held me for a long time.

'Laureth,' he said. 'I think we should stay. Stay and find Dad.'

'Is that what you really think?' I asked. I was trying not to cry again.

'Yes,' said Benjamin. 'And Laureth?'

'What?'

'Stan thinks the same.'

I laughed.

'Good. So that makes three of us, yes?'

'Yes, Laureth.'

# The Pious Poem

Sight must have its advantages. Like, I'm never going to drive a car, well not on public roads at least. But I can live with that. I've never wanted to be able to see, not really, but right then I knew that if I *could* see, I wouldn't have had to bring Benjamin with me, and then, I felt awful.

What I'd done had made him upset, and I knew I had to put it right.

Frail as I felt right then, I felt better.

'You know, I am scared,' I told Benjamin, but I

was totally calm as I said it.

'You don't seem scared,' he said.

'Never judge a book by its cover,' I said.

'You're not a book.'

'No,' I said, but talking about books, I knew we only had one asset at our disposal. 'Maybe not. Listen, get Dad's notebook out for me, will you? We need another clue. Can you flick through? There must be something else. See what you can find. I trust you. Like you said, you're not stupid.'

'Okay,' said Benjamin.

He began to read.

I waited, listening to the sounds around us.

From across the park was the roar of the big road we'd come on earlier, the Grand Concourse, I supposed. It was quieter in the park, but people came and went, cycles whished by. I heard an argument a way off, or it might just have been guys messing around.

It was still unbelievably hot, and barely a breath of wind, so that even in the shade of the tree, we were baking. I knew I had to get us something to eat, or at least another cold drink, and if Benjamin couldn't find anything, we'd have to go back to the hotel, and pray Dad came back before night-time.

I began to think about Dad and coincidence again, and about his book. Maybe Mum was right, maybe it was fair enough that she was angry with him. He *was* obsessed, it seemed to have taken over his life, as if he couldn't let it go, like an alcoholic can't let drink go. And after all these years, he had almost nothing to show for it, except a notebook of weird ideas and a title.

He'd had a title for *that* book for a long time. When he started out, the book had what you call a working title; something you're going to change to something better just as soon as you think of it.

His working title was *354*, which everyone hated, and then Dad would get upset and defensive and tell us yet again that it was only a working title. But secretly I think he liked that title a lot. It was odd, and Dad likes odd things, though you've probably worked that out by now.

Then one day, he said he had the real title of the book, which was this; *The Hound of Heaven*.

He really liked it, and was happy for about a day, until he Googled it and found that there was already something called that; a strange old poem.

Grumpily, he read the poem to us one night after

dinner. It's very, very long, and was full of words that no one uses anymore, like casement and quaffing, and a few that I'm not even sure ever existed in the first place, like dravest and vistaed.

It's a pious poem about God. It's about how, although you might try and ignore Him, and turn from Him and even flee Him, He will keep following you, faithfully, like a faithful hound follows its master, all your life. So that finally, you will realise the power of God's love and He will have been there, just behind you, all the time. Waiting for you.

It's a bit creepy if you ask me, but that's what it's about. So *The Hound of Heaven* is a metaphor; it means God's love.

Dad sulked for a couple of weeks, and then, one evening, he said he was going to use it as the title anyway.

'I like it,' he said. 'And you know, I think the Hound of Heaven could have a different meaning. It could mean coincidence too.'

'Co-inky-dinks?' said Benjamin, who was only about five at the time, and thereby coining a new word for ever.

Dad laughed.

'Yes, co-inky-dinks. Because when one happens to you, it feels like it means something. And I think what it means is that the universe is trying to tell you something, like a guide dog. Or a dog that's close to you, unseen, guiding your way through life, giving you little clues, clues in the form of coincidences. You have to work out what they mean, these clues from the universe, from the Hound of Heaven.'

'I like that idea,' I said, because it reminded me of when Harry had a trial to see if he might be suitable for a guide dog. The dog came to school and we all pounced on it, but it didn't seem to mind.

'You like it?' said Dad. He sounded happier. 'You know, all through my life, when I've been in an important time, I mean, when big things were happening, I've seen lots of coincidences. I think they're put there for us to see, to work out what they mean. To guide us.'

So that's how Dad saw it, and that's all he has to show of his book so far. Four words. And he didn't even write those himself.

## *And Third Long*

That boy on the plane, Sam, had offered me his number. I was sitting with Benjamin on the bench, melting in the heat, wishing I'd taken it after all. I was just thinking that maybe he could have come and rescued us, when my thoughts were broken as someone called out, not far away.

'Girl, what you doing there?'

'Is he talking to us?' I whispered to Benjamin, without looking up.

Someone, a man, was calling to us, to me, from

a little way off. His voice sounded old, but I wasn't sure how old.

'What you doing?'

He was coming closer.

We'd been sitting on the bench for ages, trying to make Dad's notebook give us another clue, and failing.

Benjamin kept reading pieces aloud and stopping every other sentence to ask me if I thought it meant anything.

'Keep reading,' I said, again, and again.

We had nothing.

I was trying to think about it logically. Something had brought Dad to New York. Something other than Edgar Allan Poe, I was sure. Yes, he wanted to come to the cottage, but if he'd wanted that so badly, he'd have kept his appointment. Unless . . .

Something had brought him here, something else, and I felt sure it was to do with his number. And if Dad was right about the Hound of Heaven, about how it guided people through life, then maybe it sent this old guy to us, right then.

'What you doing there? You reading?'

Now he was close, he smelled terrible, and I

guessed he must be homeless, you could smell him a mile away. You didn't need blind superhero powers to detect that. I tried to breathe through my mouth.

'Er, yes, sort of.'

'You sort of reading? What you sort of reading?'

'Er, a notebook.'

'A notebook?'

He seemed to have to repeat everything I said.

'What kind of notebook?' he added.

Benjamin had gone very quiet. I wondered if he was frightened. And that made me wonder if I should be frightened.

'Oh,' I said, trying to work out how to get out of this conversation and get him to go away. 'Oh, well, it's Dad's notebook.'

'Your pappy's?'

'Uh-huh,' said Benjamin, and that made me relax slightly, because if he'd been scared he'd have kept quiet.

'Why? What you reading it for?'

'We just are,' I said, and then I thought, well, if this guy is going to pester us, he might at least be useful.

'Can I ask you something?' I said.

'Sure you can.'

'Are you from around here?'

'You mean the Bronx?'

'Well, New York. The Bronx. Wherever we are.'

'Sure am. Why'd you wanna know?'

'Does the number 354 mean anything to you?'

'Does the number 354 mean anything to me?' he repeated.

'Yes, 354.'

'Listen, numbers are everything in this town, see? You know that? You're not from here, right? Where you from?'

'We're from London. From England.'

'London, England? I always wanted to go there. What's it like?'

'It's cold and wet. Listen, does the number 354 mean anything, anything special? In New York, I mean.'

'Well, sure. Numbers is how we get around. You know that? Like to tell someone where to meet, you say the numbers; like the corner of 85th and 3rd. Or 1-16th and 1st. Right?'

Despite the heat, I felt a chill fingertip slide its way up my neck. Or rather, I could hear the pounding of dog's feet right behind us; because this was the Hound. The Hound had come for us.

'Could you say that again?'

But Benjamin was way ahead of me.

'That's it!' he said. '35th and 4th.'

'Right!' said the man. 'Excepting. There ain't no 4th Avenue.'

My heart sank.

'There isn't,' I said. I felt sick.

'Nope. Well, there's a little bit of it. Most of it these days is called Park Avenue. Just the bit below 15th is called 4th. And everything above that is Park. So there ain't no 35th and 4th.'

'Oh,' I said.

'But that ain't the only way about,' the man went on. '354? So that's 3rd and 54th street. Right?'

'Right!' I said. I stood up, pulling Benjamin to his feet.

'Where you going? You in a hurry?'

'Yes, we are. Sorry. Thank you. Thank you so much.'

'You're welcome. You say hello to London for me, yeah? Tell it I'm coming to see it. One of these days, real soon.'

'We will,' I said. 'Thank you.'

I got Benjamin to get us back to the Grand Concourse and tell me when he saw a taxi coming, which didn't take long, and we set off for 3rd and 54th street.

It took much longer to get to the junction than it had to get a taxi, and it was gone five by the time we got there. We were both exhausted, and hungry, but we didn't want to give up. I was doing my best not to think how long we'd been up for. I was doing my best not to think about how hungry and thirsty I was, and presumably Benjamin was too. I knew we had to keep going, because the only other choice was to stop, and then we'd be done for.

We got out at 3rd and 54th.

'What do you see?' I asked Benjamin.

He didn't reply for a moment. I felt him twisting around, looking each way.

'What am I looking for?'

'I don't know,' I said. 'Just tell me what's on each corner.'

'Okay,' said Benjamin. 'There's a clothes shop, with clothes in it. There's a sports shop. There's a big building with nothing on it. I think it's houses. And there's a bar.'

'A bar? What's it called.'

'It's funny. *Third And Long*, I think. Well, that's what's on the sign on the front, anyway.'

I thought for a moment.

Third And Long. At 3rd and 54th.

There were five letters in Third. Three in And, and four in Long. It wasn't quite right, but it was very close. It should have been called *And Third Long*. But it wasn't.

'Come on,' I said.

'Dad's in the bar?' Benjamin asked.

'We'll see.'

We crossed the street and headed inside.

It was noisy. It sounded loud, and it sounded rough. There was a sports game playing on a TV or a radio, and there was the noise of lots of men shouting and joking.

A noise that died a little as we walked in.

Someone whistled, a wolf whistle.

'Laureth?' Benjamin said quietly. He was holding my hand very tightly.

'Just see if you can see Dad,' I said.

'There's loads of people.'

'I know. But can you see Dad?'

Someone whistled again and someone else called out something rude, that I prayed Benjamin didn't understand. The noise returned, men laughing and shouting.

'I can't see,' said Benjamin. 'I'll have a quick look. Don't move. I'll come back for you.'

'Wait, Benjamin!' I said, but he'd gone, and then a couple of things happened at once.

I began to panic. My little brother was somewhere in a bar of guys all drinking and having loud fun, and I didn't know where he was. That was the first thing, and the second thing was that my phone rang.

VoiceOver spoke the name of the caller to me. I didn't catch it at first, but as it spoke the second time I held it to my ear.

It was Mum.

And just as I was wondering whether to answer it or not, I dropped it.

It was so loud in the bar I couldn't hear where it landed, and I fell to my knees immediately, and began to sweep my hands around, frantically.

There was laughter, shouts.

'Hey sweetheart, take your shades off!'

'Forget that, take your clothes off!'

There was more laughter and I still couldn't find my phone. It was still ringing but in all the din I couldn't tell where it was, and I wasn't looking for it properly, not sensibly, just waving my hands around on the floor, stupidly.

'Look at her go!' laughed another man, and then Benjamin was there, kneeling on the floor next to me.

'Laureth, get up. Get up, Laureth. Dad's not here. I've looked everywhere.'

'He's not?' I said.

'I can't see him. I don't want to be in here anymore.'

He was right about that.

'But my phone . . .'

'I've got your phone,' he said. We stood up and hurried out of the bar, as fast as we could, with more dirty comments following me.

We walked down the street, without stopping for ages.

'Where are we going?' asked Benjamin.

'Away from there.'

We walked on for a bit until the desire to cry had left me, and then I remembered something.

'Give me my phone,' I said, and Benjamin hesitated.

'Give me my phone. Benjamin. What is it?'

'Please don't be cross with me,' he said, and he sounded so worried, I knew immediately what had happened.

The Benjamin Effect. My phone was dead.

# The Human Mind

'She doesn't mean to be cross,' Benjamin said.

He was talking to Stan but I knew it was for my benefit.

I sighed, heavily.

'I'm not cross,' I said. I held out my hand and after a moment Benjamin took it. I pulled him into a cuddle before he could argue, and then began tickling him and jabbing him in the ribs, till he was giggling wildly.

'Hey! Hey stop it!' he cried, laughing. 'Hey, I've dropped Stan!'

I let him go then so he could rescue the raven.

There was a sudden silence and I knew what was coming.

'Raven attack!' wailed Benjamin and suddenly Stan was in my face, flapping his wings and cawing. I laughed and did the best job I could of being pecked at by Stan.

'No! No, stop! Oh, please stop!' I said, mucking about and Stan must have been satisfied because the attack ended abruptly.

'What are we going to do now?' asked Benjamin, just like that.

I tried my phone again, but it had had its brain fried for sure.

'Well,' I said.

'Are we going to that other street corner? The one the man said? 35th and Park?'

I hesitated. I really doubted there would be anything there, and I just couldn't take any more disappointments, and I was pretty sure Benjamin couldn't either.

Maybe I had something at the back of my mind, something Dad had once said about near misses.

One day he came over to me and sat down with a

heavy thump on the sofa next to me.

'I've been thinking,' he said.

'Steady now,' I said.

'Funny girl,' he said. 'No, listen. You know the thing that really gets me about coincidences?'

'I can't imagine,' I said.

'The thing that really gets me is this; for all the times a coincidence happens, there must be just as many times when one *nearly* happens. In fact, there are probably thousands of near misses for every coincidence that does happen, but we just don't know about it.'

'Like what?'

'Well, I got back from that Swedish book fair last week, and I came through the airport. And I came home.'

'So?'

'Exactly. So what? But supposing that there was an old school-friend, someone I haven't seen in twenty years also coming back that day, and I missed him by seconds. Just around a corner, or something. Doesn't that freak you out? That idea?'

'Dad,' I said. 'I think you've been working too hard again. Or not hard enough. One of the two.'

'Maybe,' he said, and so I was thinking about near misses, and what if Dad was at that other street corner trying to count if there were 354 paving stones or something?

'Are we?' Benjamin repeated.

'No,' I said, trying to see if I felt better for making up my mind. I didn't much, but it was a decision at least.

'Why not?'

'Because we're too tired, and it's too late, and I think we ought to go back to the hotel now. We'll try tomorrow.'

'But won't we be with Dad tomorrow?'

'Yes,' I said. 'Yes. Of course.'

'I hope so,' said Benjamin, very quietly.

As we trundled along in a taxi, I held my phone, pressing the power button again and again, but there was nothing. I wanted to phone Mum back, I was desperate to speak to her, to hear her voice, and yet I couldn't blame Benjamin; he'd only wanted to get us out of that bar as fast as possible and I had wanted that too.

It had seemed to me as though the smelly tramp had been sent to us. It had seemed to me that he *was* the Hound, come to find us and nudge us on our way, but as we rode silently back to the hotel, I knew it was something else that had been at work.

I'd had a long conversation with Dad about this, a while ago, and it was something called apophenia.

There was, of course, stuff about it in The Black Book.

## APOPHENIA.

Apophenia is a fancy word, but all it means is that thing we all have inside us, a desire, a tendency, a need in fact, to spot patterns. The human mind is very good at spotting patterns.

It's an evolutionary development.

To spot faces, for example. We're so good at spotting faces, that we see them all over the place: all it takes is a line and two dots above it for us to see one. Even the front of a car, or a house with two windows above a central door, or in fact anything with two blobs and a line reminds people of a face.

To be able to quickly spot faces, and therefore friendly faces from hostile ones, would have been really important to our distant ancestors.

Other patterns would have been important too, like seeing the marks of a leopard camouflaged amongst the grass, or the spots of a jellyfish in the shallows. Maybe basic pattern recognition is even how sight started in the first place.

* * *

Patterns aren't just visual though: it must have been important to our ancestors to spot that autumn came after summer, which came after spring, so they knew when to plant things. The ability to spot the patterns of the moon and the sun must have come along around then too. All very useful. Essential in fact, if you're a caveman.

It might not seem like much, but it's a very impressive skill. One of the biggest challenges facing scientists working with Artificial Intelligence is getting a computer to spot patterns.

They've had some success, which is why Jane's got a digital camera that knows where people's faces are. She laughed when it tried to focus on that snowman Benjamin made, but the camera had spotted a face; two blobs of coal and a carrot.

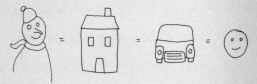

But if you try and get a computer to spot _unspecified_ patterns between things, they're almost totally useless. And yet your average five-year-old can work out the simplest connections better than the smartest computer.

That's why a small child can tell

you the connection between Santa Claus and Rudolph is that they both have something red about them, while a robot will spin around screaming 'does not compute' and 'illogical' until steam comes out its ears and it blows up.

So we've evolved to become very good at spotting patterns, and more than that, we actually LIKE to spot patterns.

We like it SO MUCH, we even do it when there isn't actually a pattern there to be spotted. We easily make one up, we find it among all the information presented to us, even if all that's in front of us is no more than random noise.

That's apophenia. Finding a pattern when it isn't really there.

And that's what Benjamin and I had just been guilty of.

We'd wanted to find meaning in the number 354, and with thousands, no wait, millions of numbers at our disposal in New York, we'd turned it into an address and duly trotted off to find out that we were deluding ourselves.

It's that same business as the birthday problem again; with enough numbers to choose from, of course you're going to find the odd coincidence sooner or later. Like Carl Jung. He got all freaked out because of what had once happened in the case of the scarab beetle and his patient. The key word in all that is 'once'. Given that he must have conducted thousands of therapy sessions in his life, it would have been more remarkable if he'd *never* experienced some kind of coincidence connected to one, wouldn't it? And to make matters worse, it wasn't even a real scarab beetle trying to get through the window, just something *like* a scarab beetle.

And yet that simple thing was enough to set Jung on a lifelong mission to find out what coincidences mean.

We could have walked back to the hotel faster than the taxi, and as we trundled long, Benjamin flicked through the notebook.

Coincidentally, you might say, the pages he read were about Jung. Jung, and some other people, including the man that Benjamin's 'effect' was named after, Wolfgang Pauli.

And what Benjamin read, I didn't like the sound of at all, not one little bit.

# THE FATAL IDEA

Needs must, I always say, and right now I NEED to find out THE TRUTH about all this so I can put it in MY DAMN BOOK!

Let's recap  AGAIN

Protagonist finds out the truth. Tips him over the edge. What is this truth? Something bad? I have been supposing that

the truth behind coincidences
is something positive, something
good. But why did I assume that?
Supposing it's not?

Something bad tips him over the
edge and leads to the inevitable.

Which is?

Think more about this . . . Still
need a plot!

* * *

There is some idea, some fatal idea
lurking. The Hound is not a force for
good, but one of destruction?

*  *  *

Jung's search for meaning.

1930: Pauli publishes major work on the neutrino, immediately has a nervous breakdown. He consults the top psychiatrist - Carl Jung.

Jung finds Pauli's dreams fascinating, and soon they begin to discuss the connections between their two apparently very different sciences; psychology and physics. They seek the connections between the mind and the universe.

Pauli becomes convinced that the link between physics and psychology is Jung's synchronicity - COINCIDENCE.

Jung and Pauli discuss the underlying nature of the universe. They believe there is a single number that explains everything, and begin to wonder if the number is the weird choice of a certain three-digit number: 137.

Pauli becomes obsessed with the number.

But Pauli's number was 137. The number is known as the FINE-STRUCTURE CONSTANT and the discovery of its true value has been the obsession of many great physicists. The fine-structure constant, 137, is critical in explaining

NOT 354?
WHY NOT?
IT HAD TO BE!

the behaviour of light, among other things.

Light is energy.

Energy, as Einstein tells us in $E=mc^2$, is the same as matter.

Therefore light IS matter and therefore EVERYTHING can be explained by the number 137.

Jung and Pauli wrote a book on the subject together, each of them writing one half. It is a book that few people understand, and one that greatly damaged Pauli's reputation as a reputable scientist.

Wolfgang Pauli

But Pauli continued to see this number underlying many values in physics, like a fingerprint. He believed it was a number with special significance in the universe, and it appeared to him continually, not only inside his lab, but outside it too.

As he pursued his hunt for the meaning of 137, his life and career sank into increasing chaos.

Towards the end of his life, he contracted cancer. He was wheeled into a hospital room. The number on the door was 137.

He told his friends he would not
be leaving the room, and they told
him he was being foolish. But he
was right. He died in room 137.

*  *  *

Other disciples of coincidence.

Albert Einstein.

Carl Jung.

Arthur Koestler.

Paul Kammerer.

Albert
Einstein

Paul
Kammerer

Today,     DECEMBER 20TH
           – NOTE!!


   I put the following initials
into the anagram server website
at http://www.wordsmith.org/
anagram/index.html
   Albert Einstein – AE
   Carl Jung – CJ
   Arthur Koestler – AK
   Paul Kammerer – PK
   There is only one result. A
result that has scared the hell out
of me. When I saw it on screen I
did not believe it. Thought someone
was playing some weird joke on
me. But the only one who could

be playing a trick on me is the universe. The Hound of Heaven.

I know about Einstein and Jung, but only a little about Koestler and Kammerer. READ MORE>

Paul Kammerer, a contemporary of Jung. Most notably a geneticist, he also developed an elaborate theory of coincidences, called The Law of Seriality. Wrote a book with the same name.

In 1926 Kammerer committed suicide. He went out into the Schneeberg forest in the Austrian Alps, put a gun to the left side of his head and pulled the trigger.

\* \* \*

Koestler also wrote a whole book on coincidence.

As he wrote it, researching Kammerer, a shower of coincidences happened to him. He thought Kammerer's ghost was guiding him.

<u>In The Roots of Coincidence</u>

he discusses probability, and its relation to apparent coincidences. He wrote about how the universe seems to stop existing at the quantum level. He discussed physics' weakness; that it only considers matter, and, as Charles Michael Kittridge Thompson IV would also do many years later, asked 'Where is my mind?'

By which he meant: what is the universe if it is not understood by a human mind? Does it exist at all?

His thoughts therefore
echo Jung and Pauli; that to
understand the universe we must
unify psychology and physics.
Mind _and_ matter.

Arthur Koestler committed
suicide in 1983. He made a suicide
pact with his wife and she killed
herself alongside him.


\* \* \*

George Price, one of America's
greatest thinkers. Also a
geneticist. Inventor of the Price
Equation.

Price began to be obsessed with coincidence. After an incredible series of coincidences happened to him, he, being a clever mathematician, calculated the odds of what had happened, and found it too much to believe.

He 'gave in and had to admit that God existed'.

As a result he had some sort of religious conversion. He walked into a church in London on 14 June 1970 and pressed the priest to give him the answers he sought.

He gave away all his money and possessions, invited tramps into his home. He also became interested in a three-digit number, though HIS number was 666. An infamous number, popularly known as THE NUMBER OF THE BEAST, though Price believed it had a true and hidden meaning.

He calmly committed suicide in 1975, opening his carotid artery with a pair of nail scissors. He put a note on the bathroom door warning whoever it was that would find him.

In his suicide note, he quoted from a poem.

The poem was The Hound of Heaven.

## Two Dried Mice


That passage in the Black Book horrified me.

Benjamin didn't understand everything he was reading. In fact, neither did I, but I understood enough to become seriously worried.

Benjamin was still reading as the taxi reached the hotel, and he finished the notebook sitting on the bed, with me sitting next to him, half wondering why I could still hear the sounds of New York in the street below, when all I should have been wondering about was whether Dad had followed the path of those other men, those other men who'd become obsessed with coincidence, and had ended up taking their own lives.

I wanted to scream, and to cry, but I couldn't do either.

Benjamin was talking to Stan, just chatting away as if nothing odd was happening. I couldn't believe he was still awake; I was exhausted, I wanted to curl up and sleep and pray that when I woke up, it had all been the strangest dream, and nothing more.

'Is that it?' I asked Benjamin.

'I told you,' he said. 'That's the end of the notebook. There's nothing more than that. The end.'

'What was that web address? In the notebook?'

Benjamin sighed.

'You said we'd get some food. There's a café. Just down there. We could go there.'

'Yes,' I agreed. 'I promise. Just point me towards Dad's laptop first, will you?'

'Okay, Laureth,' Benjamin said, and I realised, once again, not only how much I needed Benjamin, but how much I loved him too.

I booted up Dad's MacBook and had Benjamin read me that web address.

I entered the initials Dad had put into it; Albert

Einstein AE, Paul Kammerer PK, Carl Jung CJ, Arthur Koestler AK.

I hit enter, and before I could even tab VoiceOver through to read me the result, Benjamin saw it.

'Why's Dad's name on the screen?' he asked.

I went cold.

I didn't understand what was going on, I didn't understand what was in Dad's mind, or what all these strange things I was reading about meant. I wanted someone to help me, to tell me it was okay, and that nothing, absolutely nothing was wrong.

'Why's Dad's name there?'

'Is that it?' I asked. 'The result of that anagram?'

'Yes. That's weird. Why did you put those letters in?'

'Never mind,' I said.

I stood up. 'Let's go and get some food, shall we?'

'Yay!' said Benjamin. 'Stan says . . . '

'Actually,' I said. 'Wait. There's one last thing I want to do while we have the laptop on.'

Benjamin groaned and took Stan over to the window.

'See that café, Stannous?' he said. 'Soon. Very soon, you, me and my big sister will go there and eat something. Would you like that? You would? Oh, good!'

While Benjamin spoke to Stan, I checked my emails. Maybe Mum had sent me a message when she couldn't get through on the phone. Maybe Dad had.

I felt empty inside. Done. And suddenly I knew it was time to give in. I decided to write to Mum and ask her to come and get us.

'Well, Stan, what do you think of Dad's book? Weird, isn't it?'

I heard Benjamin move away from the window and sit on the bed again, and I heard pages turning.

I logged into my email.

There was nothing new from anyone. Just some junk mail.

'Very weird, indeed,' Benjamin said to Stan. 'If this is how you make a book I don't think I want to be a writer when I grow up.'

I was about to write the email to Mum when out of habit, I logged into Dad's email too, and that's when I found the email from Mr Walker, from Michael.

It was recent, sent since we'd met him earlier in the day, and what it said was this:

*My dear Laureth,*

*There's something I should have said about your dad's notebook. To be honest it is a matter that I found too peculiar to credit at first, but I've been pondering it all afternoon and I find I am unable to remain silent. If you are free this evening I would ask if you and your charming brother could meet me at eight o'clock, on the corner of Nobell Street and Baisley Boulevard, in Queens. It would be easier to show you than to explain.*

*Yours sincerely, Mr Michael Walker.*

So I knew it was him all right. No one else I knew spoke like that. I went to check my phone and then remembered it was dead.

'What time is it?' I asked Benjamin, but he didn't answer. I thought about the email I had been about to write, and felt a tiny speck of determination inside me. If I gave up now, not only would Mum be furious, I'd have failed too. She was going to be furious anyway, but I wanted to find Dad first. Myself.

'Benjamin! What time is it?'

'Hmm?' he said. 'What? Oh, it's seven . . . I mean seven . . . fifteen.'

'We have to go!' I said.

'Food?'

'We'll get something to take away,' I said. 'Come on.'

I sent a quick reply to Mr Walker and we headed downstairs again, and happily this time Benjamin helped me avoid the tricky one.

'It's spooky here now,' he said.

'What is?'

'It's so dark now, it's like being in a scary film.'

'What? The corridor?'

'The whole hotel.'

'Maybe they don't like their electricity bills.'

'Too cool for school, that's what Dad would say.'

'You said.'

'I know I did. I'm saying it again.'

We managed to get out of the hotel and across the street in one piece, and into the café.

Benjamin steered me to the counter and I asked him what he wanted.

'A cheese sandwich, please. And Stan will have a dried mouse.'

'I'll see if they have any.'

'Actually he says he'd like two dried mice.'

It turned out that it's not so simple to ask for two cheese sandwiches in a New York deli, so it took a long three-way conversation to discuss what kind of bread we wanted, and what kind of cheese and what we wanted on the cheese and about a hundred other things. The man behind the counter was very patient and friendly, but I was worried about the time, and meeting Mr Walker. Fortunately it was easy enough to buy two cans of Coke, but all the while I was talking to the man, something was bothering me, something unpleasant. And that was on top of a bit of me that was screaming the words 'please don't let Dad have killed himself' over and over and over, at full volume.

'Do they have mouse?' asked Benjamin.

'No, I don't think so.'

'Did you ask?'

'Not in so many words.'

'Well, please can you ask? Because Stan is hungry.'

I smiled towards the man behind the counter and said in a loud voice, 'Do you have any dried mice for my brother's raven? Please?'

The man laughed.

'Not since the hygiene inspector last paid a call. There you go, sweetheart. Fourteen-eighty.'

Then I realised what was making me feel uncomfortable; there was a bad smell of smoke. You don't smell it often but when you do it's horrible, the smell of a chain smoker, a smoker who never changes their clothes or washes their hair. Who reeks of ashtrays, days old. It made me want to get out of the café and I told Benjamin to take our stuff while I was paying.

Benjamin made an odd noise and something hit the floor.

'Did you drop something?' I asked.

'Uh-huh,' said Benjamin.

'What? What have you brought?'

'Stan,' said Benjamin.

'Stan doesn't sound like a book when you drop him.'

Benjamin picked whatever it was up and held my hand.

'Please can you carry our drinks,' he said, 'because

I already have Stan and the sandwiches.'

'And?'

'And . . . Dad's notebook. Laureth, there's something else in it.'

'There's *what*? You said we'd got to the end.'

'I know. But Dad did something weird.'

'What? What did he do?'

'He wrote in the back of it too. There's something in the back of it. Something weird.'

'In the back?' I said. I wanted to scream, but I managed not to. 'In the back? Why didn't you see it before? Why didn't you look in the back before?'

'You didn't ask me to,' said Benjamin. Then in a small voice he added, 'I don't like you when you're cross.'

I bit my tongue and waited a moment, and tried to remember that Benjamin was only seven, and that I had abducted him, that he was up way past anyone's bedtime, let alone his, and that no one might ever forgive me for any of this anyway.

'Sorry,' I said. I wanted to hug him but my hands were full. 'I'm not cross. You're doing really well. Really.'

So we got out of the deli and the bellhop at The

Black King called another taxi for us.

'Busy day you guys are having,' he said. There was a tightness to his voice and I wondered if he knew what Margery Lundberg had planned for us; a crocodile pit, perhaps, or a death ray of some kind.

'Uh-huh,' I said, and we headed for Queens, while Benjamin, in between slurps of Coke and mouthfuls of cheese sandwich, read what he'd found in the back of Dad's notebook.

Benjamin was right. If there had been odd things already, this was the oddest of all, and the most frightening by far.

# THE FINAL CLUE

It's awful, what she finds here: the truth bare and naked upon the earth. They are truly here: The Death Cult. The Hound. Both are truly real.

Men guard this, the truth. They are known with the awful name; The Death Cult. The Hound? Some dog! That's just the coded name for their evil; the gangs they use, which hide the truth.

Well, I've found what Poe found.

What did Pauli find? And Price?

- That the truth sets the Hound free.

The Hound runs, and kills.

Each and every good man: smart, wise and noble.

Each one slain.

Each sad death, fake; all faked, like the idiot went mad.


Every time, the Hound runs, and kills. Once it's shown prey, the howls will fly right over the world. More and older dogs now chase down the paths that you hurry over. The

eager dogs run after your wet heels;
they are close, hard and cruel.

Flee, you think! Flee! But you'll
fail, and these evil men shall come and
break your ego. Maybe kill you. Cause
your own death. Kill you stone dead
but truly make you think that you
ended your own silly life.

*  *  *

I've found just one thing; they, the
death cult, are truly here and truly
real.

Run!

Would that you could.

Wish for other, good men; noble folk who fight them, but there, Fool, you shall fail.

\* \* \*

But maybe, when she finds this, the truth will set loose over the world, hunt the Hound down and throw that fey beast onto the dirty soil.

\* \* \*

The clues that I've found must now reach over the world. When she finds that the Black Book has every fact, and every last lie that's kept the truth from our sight, when she reads what I've found, when she tells good

men about what The Death Cult set
loose upon the world, then all shall
know the truth.

* * *

When I've truly gone, she might weep,
and she'll feel the sting that hot
tears give sad, tired eyes. But tears
mean one thing; that you loved well,
and others love you still, even now
you're gone.

## God Plays Dice

'Trust me' is another thing Mum says a lot and it must be one of the most worrying things ever to say. If someone says 'trust me' to you, you basically know it's probably a really bad idea to do just that.

'I don't want to go out again,' Benjamin said, and for once he sounded every bit like an overtired seven-year-old.

But what we had to do right then was get a taxi out of Manhattan and back into Queens as night fell.

'Trust me,' I said. 'It'll be fine.'

There was a short gap before he said, 'Okay,

Laureth.' A short gap that freaked me out more than anything had so far, because it meant my little brother had stopped trusting me, and that made me really sad.

I didn't want to have Benjamin read those pages again; those two strange pages at the back of Dad's notebook. But I didn't need him to anyway, they were seared into my brain, and each time I heard the words in my head I felt smaller and smaller, and despite the wondrousness of Benjamin and Stan, I felt utterly, totally alone. The words were stilted, and forced, yet somehow poetic, but I didn't care about that. What I cared about was what it suggested about Dad's *state of mind*. Which was that he had lost it. Completely.

What was Dad talking about? A cult? A death-dealing cult hiding the truth? That those who'd come close to finding out the truth about coincidences had been killed, and their deaths made to look like suicides? Kammerer, Koestler? Price, maybe even Pauli and Poe? This was Dad's life, Dad's *real* life. Had he really discovered some weird truth about the world, the universe? Had the cult got him?

And who was 'she' in the text? I couldn't shift the feeling that 'she' was me.

And I was just a stupid girl whose brain was

melting trying to figure it all out. Dad had said the Hound was a metaphor for coincidences, positive things that guide you; good things. Now he seemed to be saying the Hound, and therefore coincidences too, were evil.

Was that fact or fiction in the back of his notebook? Did he even know the difference anymore?

$$\sim\!\sim\!\!\curlyvee$$

What it seemed to come down to was this; either you believed that coincidences have some secret, hidden meaning, a secret that caused many of these great minds to put an end to themselves, or they are simply chance happenings.

Einstein's view was God does not play dice, by which he meant that the universe operates to a fixed set of rules. The rules might be very complicated, but if you could discover them all and understand them, then you could predict everything and anything. Imagine balls pinging around on a pool table. It might be very hard to do the maths, but if you were able to, you'd be able to predict exactly where every ball would end up even if you smashed one into a whole bunch of them and they all went flying.

But if that's the case, then Einstein must have been saying that there is no such thing as chance. Everything follows rules. And if *that's* the case, then coincidences aren't chance either. They must mean something; there must be a hidden reason behind even the most extravagant coincidences, because if you take the other option, and coincidences are just chance, and have no meaning, that would mean that God does play dice.

And I don't think Albert Einstein can have been wrong, can he?

⌇⌇⌇

I thought about how Pauli died in the room with his special number on it and I thought about Dad and *his* special number, and I wanted to scream at him one very simple question:

Why does it matter, why the hell do you care?

Because I really didn't.

I just wanted Dad to be okay. I wanted him not to have gone crazy, not to have done something stupid, something that meant he wouldn't be coming back to the hotel that night, or in fact, any night.

I think Benjamin fell asleep in the taxi, because

300

when I asked him if he was okay, there was no reply. I put my hand out and felt him curled up on the seat next to me. I felt his messy hair and I felt Stan tucked up under his chin, and I felt bad. I'd dragged him across the world and all around the city all day on not much more than a cheese sandwich.

The taxi ride was a long one, and I was beginning to wonder how much longer it was going to take when Benjamin woke up.

'Oh!' he said. 'Look, Stan. We're on TV!'

I thought he was messing around at first, but he tugged my arm.

'Laureth! We're on TV!'

'We are?' I asked, confused. Perhaps he'd been dreaming it. 'Where?'

'On the little TV. That picture of you and me. The one Dad took at Christmas at Grandma's. But the sound's off . . . '

'Don't you touch it!' I said. 'I'll put the sound on, Benjamin. Just tell me where to touch.'

So he did, but it took a second or two, and we were only in time to hear the end of a news story.

' . . . could be anywhere in the city. Officials from Customs and Border Protection at JFK are facing a barrage of questions, raising the issue of how the two British children were able to pass through the airport earlier today.'

The voice of the TV announcer changed tone. It had been official and serious. Now she went all soft and gentle.

'So please, folks. If you see these two missing children, do the right thing and put them in touch with the police, or other suitably secure professionals. Remember, the elder child is a blind girl of just sixteen. She'll be terrified at being lost in our big city. Alone with just her kid brother. They'll be completely helpless.'

I sat, speechless, while the news announcer rattled on.

'Sports news! The Jets today revealed the name . . . '

'Wow,' said Benjamin. 'We're famous! Sorry you weren't in the photo too, Stan. Never mind, maybe there'll be another one with you in later.'

'Can the driver hear that thing?' I whispered.

Benjamin thought for a minute.

'I don't know. I don't think so. He's just driving.'

'Good,' I said. 'Good.'

I thought frantically, trying to work out what it

meant. How did they know we were here? I knew they would have our names as having passed through immigration that afternoon, but why would anyone think we were missing, unless someone had told them?

And how did anyone *know* we were missing? I'd had that phone call from Mum a couple of hours before, but how did she know we were missing? And even if she did, how did she know we were in New York?

There was no time to answer any of these thoughts, because our journey had come to an end.

The taxi lurched to a stop, swinging into the kerb at the last second.

'Thirty-five forty,' said the taxi driver.

I almost shouted at him.

'What?'

'Hey lady, don't blame me for the night rate. Take it up with the mayor. Thirty-five dollars and forty cents.'

'No,' I said. 'No, you see. It's just that—'

'Laureth,' said Benjamin. 'Pay him. I can see Michael waiting for us.'

I pulled a fifty-dollar note from my left-hand

pocket and handed it to the driver, but I was freaked out. Dad's number was chasing us. And if the number was, then maybe the Hound was too.

The driver gave me the change and we got out. It was much quieter than Manhattan, at the hotel. It was still hot, although I knew the sun had gone down. I heard another car or two on the street, further up, but otherwise everything was pretty peaceful.

Benjamin held my hand and took me over to Michael.

'Laureth, Benjamin,' he announced, still in that posh voice of his. 'So good to see you again.'

'You too, Michael,' I said. 'What's this all about?'

I wondered if he had seen us on TV.

'You know,' he said, 'I've been wondering about your name. It's most unusual.'

'It's Welsh,' I said. 'Did you bring us all the way out here to ask that? I thought you—'

'No, no,' he said. 'There is another matter. It concerns your father's notebook.'

'And?'

'And, well, I had the opportunity to look over it, when I found it. It was very peculiar, but there was one thing that troubled me somewhat. Puzzled me, I should perhaps say.'

'Which was?'

'I noted that your father is interested in the phenomenon of coincidence, correct?'

'You could say that.'

Or, I thought, you could say he's lost his mind, and maybe even more than that.

'I noticed that he seems fascinated by a certain number, perhaps you're aware of that.'

'Yes,' I said. 'Three hundred and fifty-four. What about it?'

'I wanted to show you something. I live just over there. I go to school, when I deem it absolutely necessary to do so, right here.'

He hesitated and I knew what was going on. It's a silence I've come to recognise, a silence which means that someone has just realised they're trying to get a blind person to look at something, and has become deeply embarrassed as a result. Sometimes that embarrassment makes them angry, as if it's my fault, but not this time. Mr Michael Walker knew how to operate.

'I'm so sorry. The details of these two things are

irrelevant. What *is* important, and what concerns us, is my school. Maybe Benjamin can read the sign to you, so you know I'm not fabricating anything. Benjamin?'

'It's dark, I can't . . . Oh, yes, wait. Hey! That's funny.'

'What's so funny?' I asked.

'Michael's school. It's called Public School 354. That's Dad's number again!'

'Yes, you see, that's what I found so peculiar,' said Michael and he began to explain again about finding the book, and emailing me.

It was the Hound again, on our heels.

'There's something else,' Michael said. 'I remembered something else about when I found the notebook.'

'You did?' I asked. 'What?'

'There was a train passing at the time.'

'So?'

'Well the book might have come from the train. The place I go to is under the railroad track, in some trees by the bridge on Baisley. I searched my memory with great scrutiny and now that I have, there was a train passing overhead at the time.'

'The book came from the train?' I said.

Did that mean Dad had been on the train? Or just his book? It raised a whole new set of questions and I was feeling slightly mad that Michael hadn't mentioned it before, but right then, things went seriously bad.

I heard footsteps approaching.

They stopped, and Michael stopped mid-sentence.

Then I heard Benjamin say, 'Oh, wow, that looks just like a real knife.'

I heard a voice I didn't know.

'Get lost. Yes, you. I don't want your kind sticking your filthy nose in our little business here. I said get out of here!'

I heard Michael make a funny noise in his throat and then I heard him scurry away.

I smelled the smell of smoke. Stale smoke, rancid and old, like an ashtray breathing all over me, and I knew we'd been followed.

## The Wrong Idea

'Love you.'

As we stood in the street in Queens, facing a stranger with a knife, I remembered the very last thing Dad had said to me the final time I saw him. As I'd got out of the car that Sunday night, as I'd hurried away, he'd told me he loved me. And I hadn't replied.

All I could think was *please let me get to tell him*. Please, please, please.

Most of the time, despite the saying, *fiction* is stranger than *fact*. But then, every once in a while, real life gets spectacularly messed up.

Dad was right. There really was a secret about coincidences, and there really was a cult of violent men spread across the world whose job it was to protect that secret. To kill, and to make the deaths appear as suicides.

And one of those men was standing in front of us, with a knife.

Or so it seemed.

Then, just when I thought I had understood that, it got even more confusing, because the smoky man started to talk to us.

'Good. That's better, right? We don't want his kind interfering with our business, right?'

His voice was lower than before, and he was acting as though we were friends, but I knew it was an act. I pulled Benjamin into my side, and he clung to me like a limpet. I felt Stan squashed up against me.

'Listen—'

'No, you listen. You listen up, and let me do the talking, right?'

I heard fumbling noises, a match striking, and he sucked on a cigarette.

'Goddammit,' he said. 'That's better. Can't smoke anywhere in this damn city now. Can't smoke in the deli, can't smoke in the yellow cab . . . '

'Are you okay?' I whispered to Benjamin, who was frozen to my side, and I knew he knew it was a real knife.

'He's good,' said the Smoke. 'Real good. So. You two are famous, right? There we were wondering what to do next, when you walked into the deli, which was very helpful, right?'

'What do you want?' I managed to get out.

'Shut up,' he said, and now his voice was the nasty one he'd used with Michael. 'I'll tell you want I want. I want the number to the safe.'

'The safe . . . ?' I said, feeling the latest in a long line of weird things start to creep up the back of my beck.

'Don't play smart,' he said. 'You wanna go home, right? Well, you can, see? And all you gotta do is tell me the number to the safe.'

'Yes,' I said. 'Yes, I will. But I don't know which safe you're talking about.'

'I said don't play smart!'

Then Benjamin squealed and I guessed he'd waved the knife in his direction.

'We know which room you're in now. We spent

311

the whole goddamn day sitting in that Eyetie deli watching the third floor, 'cos I knew you weren't on the second. Just wanted to know which room your old man was in and then you guys show up in the deli. Seen you earlier, right? Through the window, right? And then there you are. On the television. Little lost Brits, famous old man. The girl is blind . . . So we know which room, and don't play smart anymore.'

I felt anything but smart.

'We're in room 354,' I said. 'You're right.'

'Laureth!' cried Benjamin.

'Shh,' I said. I just wanted to tell the man something, something that would make it look as though I was helping, something that would calm him down, because every now and then his voice went dark and I could only think about that knife, and Benjamin, and me.

'Do what your sister tells you, right?' he said, and Benjamin pushed himself even further into my side. 'So we picks your old man up on the Providence train. Heard him mouthing off about the fortune he's got stashed in his safe. So we got him, the phone, wallet, right? And we got his room card, so we know the hotel, only it don't have the room number on it. So we don't know the number. Not till you showed up. So just tell me the freaking code to the freaking safe and you can run along home. Minus your money and your phone. Right?'

I heard the man suck on his cigarette and blow out a long breath.

Then he screamed.

'Now!'

'I don't know,' I shouted, desperately. I was shaking physically. I started to cry and Benjamin squeezed even further into my side. 'I'm sorry. I don't know. But Dad hasn't got a fortune anyway. He's not rich.'

'I said don't play—'

He stopped.

Another voice cut in. There were footsteps, more than one set. The voice said, 'Well, bro, you goin' to cut us all?'

'Hey, now,' said the Smoke.

'You hurt *anyone* here,' said another voice, 'and you don't walk out.'

Benjamin was pulling my hand.

'It's Michael!' he whispered. 'It's Michael. He's got some friends with him!'

I could tell that.

'Hey, I was just having a little—'

'Shut your mouth,' said another voice. 'Michael here said you was rude to him. He said you don't like our kind. Is that right?'

'No, no,' said the Smoke, and now he was scared. 'Now, fellas . . .'

'Put the knife down,' said the third voice. 'Put the knife down and your wallet and your phone and then you can walk outta here. Let me tell you something. I don't like people who are mean to my kid brother.'

I felt someone take my hand.

'It's me, Laureth,' Michael said. 'Come away.'

'Michael! Who are you with?'

'My brother. His friends. I went to find them.'

I let Michael guide me away from the Smoke and the others.

'That's it,' said Michael's brother, 'on the floor it goes. Now then, my friend . . .'

I heard a soft thud and the sound of air coming out of someone all at once.

'You take your damn filthy tongue outta here, right?'

There was another thud and I heard the Smoke scream.

'What's happening?' I shouted. 'Don't! Stop it!'

'Girl, he pulled a knife on you. Hell, he pulled a knife on Michael! And my little brother might be weird, but he's still my brother, right? So this hater is gonna—'

'No!' I cried. 'Please don't! This is all bad anyway. Please don't do anything to him. Please.'

'Laureth,' said Michael. 'I don't think we ought to interfere . . . '

'No!' I said. 'No. I don't want you to hurt him.'

'We ain't gonna kill him. Just make him think twice.'

'Please!' I said. 'Please. I want to ask him something.'

'You what?'

'Please?'

Michael's brother paused, then said, 'Go right ahead.'

'You,' I called out. 'You. Did you hurt my Dad? Is he okay?'

There was silence and then another thump.

'Answer her!' said someone, and then he did.

'He's okay. He'll be walking back from Providence for a while, but we didn't touch him.'

'I don't like this,' said one of Michael's friends.

'Look,' I said, 'please don't do anything bad. What's in his wallet? Is there some ID? We can report him.'

There was a long pause, and the only thing I could hear was the Smoke groaning, lying on the ground somewhere.

'Aw . . . ' said Michael's brother. 'Aw, hell, okay. But we're taking his stuff, or he's not going anywhere.'

I thought about that. I had to admit it seemed a good idea. I wanted to get back to our room as soon as possible, but I didn't want this guy on the loose, coming after us.

'Hey, you can't take all my stuff. How'm I gonna get home?'

'You shoulda thought of that,' said Michael's brother. He sounded pretty tough.

'Come on. Give me something. Ten dollars or something.'

'Is he kidding?' said someone else. 'He's kidding, right?'

'I tell you what,' I said. 'They're going to keep your wallet and your money. But you can have your phone back.'

'What?' cried Michael's brother. 'You crazy?'

'It's okay,' I said. 'Benjamin, pick the man's phone up and give it back to him. When you're ready, Benjamin. Yes? Trust me.'

Trust me. I could have thought of something better to say, but Benjamin only took a moment to understand. He left my side, and I heard a click as he scraped the phone off the tarmac.

'Right, Benjamin?'

'Right, Laureth.'

Benjamin came back to my side, and gave me a squeeze.

'The Benjamin Effect is in operation,' he whispered.

'I still say we don't let him walk outta here,' someone said, but then it didn't matter what we thought, because there was the sound of a police siren, and someone else yelled, 'Someone's called it in. Come on . . .'

'What about him?'

'Tie the sucker to the school gates with his belt. He can explain what he's doing there.'

Michael grabbed my wrist.

'You don't want an interview with the police

department just now, do you?' he said.

'No,' I said, 'I want to get back to the hotel. I want to find Dad before they arrest us and send us home. And I want to know what's in his safe.'

'So come along,' said Michael, and he, Benjamin, Stan and I hurried away down some small alleyway he knew, heading for the main street, just as the police car wailed up to the gates of PS 354.

# The Noisy City

And then, just as Michael found a taxi for us, I suddenly wanted to ask him something.

'Michael,' I said. 'What did he mean?'

'I'm sorry, Laureth,' he said, in that way of his. 'I don't understand.'

'The man. The man with the knife. What did he mean, when he said "your kind"?'

I heard a car glide up to the kerb.

'Your taxi's here,' Michael said. 'What did he mean? Laureth, he meant because I'm black.'

'You're black?' I said, stupidly.

'Yes,' he said. 'Does that matter to you?'

'I couldn't care less if you were green with pink spots. Why would it matter to me? I don't even know what colour is.'

He thought about that.

'Listen, this gentleman surely won't wait for ever,' he said. 'But I wonder . . . Did you assume I was white?'

'Michael, I didn't assume you were anything. Try to understand, I don't see the world. I don't see colours, so I don't think about it that way at all.'

'It's most fascinating,' said Michael. 'It's a very different way of . . . '

He hesitated.

'Of what? Of seeing things? It's okay, you can say that, it doesn't offend me. I say it all the time. Yes, it's a different way of seeing things.'

'But what must your world be like?' he asked. 'What do you make of this city, how do you understand it?'

The taxi driver honked his horn, but I ignored him.

I stepped over to Michael, and put my hands over his eyes.

'Like this,' I said. 'Just listen. What do you hear?'

'The traffic,' he said.

'Yes. There's the traffic, but you can hear sounds in it, can't you? There's that big truck rumbling down there, and someone's impatient with someone over there, a little honk on the horn. And there's a loose manhole right near us. And there's more sirens in the distance, though the one for our man has stopped now. And there's a helicopter overhead, and a plane even higher than that. There's a guy selling bottles of water for a dollar down the street, and someone's just walked by with a dog, a small dog. And I haven't even *started* on the smells yet.'

I felt his cheeks lift into a smile under my hands.

'And now we really had better go,' I said.

'Laureth!' he said. 'Email me? Please?'

I smiled.

'I will!'

∿↲

Benjamin and I scrambled into the taxi, heading towards what?

Another gate to be passed? I was desperate for Dad to be on the other side.

'What did we go there for?' Benjamin asked. 'Was that man really going to hurt us?'

'No,' I said, quickly. 'Of course not. He just wanted to scare us.'

'How do you know that?'

'I . . . I don't. I'm guessing. But listen, Benjamin. He said he hadn't hurt Dad! Dad's okay. But he's lost somewhere.'

'Providence,' said Benjamin.

'What?'

'That's what the man said. He said Providence. Is that a place?'

'I'm not sure,' I said. 'I think it might be.'

'Are we going to go to Providink and find him?'

'Providink? You're silly. Yes,' I said. 'We're going to do that. Tomorrow.'

'But—'

'It's too late tonight. We need sleep. And I want to open that safe.'

I wanted, I needed, to open it, because I was now convinced Dad had put something in there that'd got him into trouble.

'But how will we open it without a key?'

'They don't have keys, they have code numbers.'

'But we don't know the code number.'

'I think we probably do,' I said, and I heard Benjamin chuckle.

'Oh, yes,' he said.

ᒣᒎᒍᒷ

The taxi pulled up and we hurried inside.

'If you see a woman who looks like she's called Margery then keep us away from her,' I said, squeezing Benjamin's hand.

The noise in the lobby was louder than ever. There was dance music playing and it sounded more like a nightclub than anything else now.

'Right,' shouted Benjamin. 'How will I know?'

'You just will. In fact, get us to the lift as fast as you can.'

'Don't worry,' he said. 'No one's going to see us in this lot.'

'What do you mean?'

'It's really busy. And dark. The whole place is packed.'

The lift doors slid closed and the noise lessened.

'Maybe Margery Lundberg will have forgotten about us,' I said. 'We can put the Do Not Disturb sign on the door and maybe she'll leave us alone.'

∽∾

We headed down the corridor and I fished out our room key, and felt glad that Michael's brother had taken the Smoke's stuff, and with it, presumably, Dad's copy of the room key. Or so I assumed. Which was why I was about to get another lesson with the help of Mum's theory, the one about learning things the hard way. I was about to learn how dangerous assumptions can be.

We went into the bedroom and Benjamin sighed.

'I'm going to bed,' he said.

'Okay,' I said. 'Where's the safe?'

He rummaged around the room for a while, and then I heard a cupboard door slide open.

'It's here. On the floor in the cupboard.'

'Okay,' I said. I knelt in front of the safe. I found the keypad. The centre number always has a little bump on it, and that's the five.

I typed 354. Nothing.

Benjamin was standing next to me.

'That can't be it,' he said. 'It wants four numbers.'

'Four?' I said. 'But . . . but we don't know a

four-digit number.'

*How do you get from three to four?* I thought, feeling as tired as poor Benjamin sounded.

In Dad's case, you got from 3 to 4 by putting a 5 in the middle. 354. But I still didn't see how to make a four-digit number out of the three-digit one that I had and still keep its value.

A siren screamed past, down in the street below, and I heard Benjamin fiddling with the blinds on the window.

'Laureth,' he said.

'Shh,' I said. 'I'm trying to think.'

I was trying some random numbers, but every time the safe made a cross buzzing sound and the door stayed shut.

'Er, Laureth,' said Benjamin. 'Please.'

'Shh!' I said.

'Laureth!' he yelled. 'There's a man coming. He's crossing the street. He was in the café, I mean the deli. He was with that smoky man. I saw them earlier because they laughed at me when I dropped Dad's book. He's heading this way. Laureth! He's just come into the hotel!'

'Oh no,' I said. 'No.'

I thought about the noisy entrance lobby. Dark and full of people. No one would notice a man heading upstairs. I thought about the Smoke, and how I had assumed that he had Dad's room card. I thought about how the Smoke had said 'we' a couple of times, and how I hadn't picked up on that. Till now.

And I thought about the safe, and whatever it was these two men wanted out of it.

And then I thought about Benjamin.

'Benjamin,' I said. I tried to sound as calm as I could. 'I want you to do something. Quickly.'

'What?'

'How many light bulbs are in this room?'

'Two. No, three.'

'And the corridor outside?'

'Only a couple, I told you, it's so—'

'I want you to smash all the bulbs in here. And the sitting room. And then I want you to go into the corridor, and smash every bulb you can see. And then I want you to run to the stairs and hide in the corridor on the second floor.'

'Smash them? Really?'

He sounded kind of excited but I knew we only had seconds to play with.

'Do it! Now! Find something hard and smash them. It has to be as dark as you can make it.'

'Right!' he said, and seconds later I heard the bulbs shattering as he clattered them with something hard and heavy-sounding.

He went next door and did the same and then he ran back in, and in the dark he fell over the bed.

'What arc you doing?' I hissed, and then he found me, shoving something soft into my hands.

'Look after Stan for me!' he whispered.

My heart pounded harder.

'I promise! I promise! Just go! Hurry!'

He stumbled away. He called out 'Bye Laureth!' in such a happy and excited way that I wanted to just howl with pain, and then I heard the distant pop of another bulb as our door shut with an ominous and very final click.

I felt for the safe again.

How to make three into four?

How to make 354 into a four-digit version of itself?

I counted seconds in my head, trying to remember how long it took the lift to come, and how long to get to the third floor. I prayed that Benjamin had finished his work and was safely somewhere on the second floor.

354 . . .

And then I had it. There is, of course, a four-digit number that is the same as 354, and that number is 0354.

I tapped the keypad once again, and the safe made a satisfied little beep and swung open. I fished around inside, and that's when I heard a plastic card slide into the lock outside, and the sound of the door opening.

# One Giant Leap

Faith. I needed it then, more than ever. It took every bit of nerve I had to send Benjamin away, but as soon as the man spoke, I knew I'd been right to.

'That's right, sugar.'

His voice made me want to weep with fear. It was a voice that was hard, a voice that belonged to someone who knew just what he was doing, and I knew immediately that this was the man to really be scared of. The Smoke was probably just his sidekick. *This* guy wasn't messing around, but at least I knew he hadn't run into Benjamin.

'That's right,' he said, slowly. 'I know you're in here.'

I heard him try the light switch.

He grunted.

'Whole floor's down, huh? Never mind. You and me can still have a good time together. In the dark.'

My hand closed over the contents of the safe. It was paper, a single large envelope, flat, as if there were nothing much inside.

The door clicked shut.

'So? You gonna come out, or shall I come in and find you?'

I said nothing. My breathing sounded so loud I couldn't believe he couldn't hear me, even though he was still in the other room and I was in the bedroom.

I leant back on my heels, and slowly stood, taking an age over it, listening for sounds of him from next door. His voice was coming closer. I remembered dimly how I'd started shaking when the Smoke had threatened us and I tried to keep calm, because I knew there was no one to help me this time. Not Michael or his friends. Not even Benjamin. And not Dad.

'I saw you come in here. Saw you from across the street, sugar. You won't get away from me. '

I heard him take a couple of steps, heard a chair tumble over.

'Goddammit,' he said, and stopped moving. 'Ow.'

I didn't move. I could barely think. Fear seemed to have rooted me to the spot.

'Now, look, sugar. Why don't you just give me the stuff, and hell, I'll even make it easy on you. Won't hurt you or nothing. Sixteen, huh? Sweet sixteen . . . Mmmm.'

His voice trailed off into a horrible moan, and I wanted to be sick.

'They said you was blind. You sure fooled us. Had no idea. Not at first. Then we saw the way you was with that brother of yours. But you do pretty good, you'd never know. Unless you was looking out for it.'

He was coming closer still as he spoke, moving slowly and stealthily this time.

'Let's get a little bit of light on the subject,' he said. I heard the roller blinds in the other room clatter up.

And then I really panicked. There must have been enough light from the street in the other room for him to see well enough.

I thought about the layout of the bedroom, where I was. The door was on the far side of the bed from me, where I stood by the safe. The window had blinds just like the sitting room.

'Hello, sugar,' he said from the doorway to the bedroom. I still didn't know for sure if he could see me or not, but I guessed he couldn't or he'd have been on me.

He took a step inside, and walked straight into the edge of the bed, which was solid metal.

'Give me the stuff!' he roared. I heard him scrambling around the side of the bed.

I leaped onto it, straight across, and felt his hand grab my ankle. I was lying on the bed, still clutching the envelope, and then I kicked out wildly with my free leg. My heel hit something that was sort of hard and soft at the same time, there was a crunch, and he yelled, really loud.

He let go of my ankle. I flung myself off the bed and ran into the other room, straight for the door.

As I opened it I heard him clattering into more furniture, but my hand was already on the door handle and I was running along the corridor for the stairs.

At the last second, I remembered the stupid way the stairs started in the floor of the corridor itself, and forced myself to slow down, find the edge, and then hurried down the wooden steps.

I heard him running after me, down the corridor.

He wasn't speaking anymore. He was making noises, grunting, like an animal running wildly, and that scared me even more.

I prayed Benjamin had taken out any lights in the stairwell too, and then I knew he had.

I was almost two flights down when I heard a scream. It was followed by a series of terrible thuds and thumps as the man fell down the long wooden staircase. And then there I was, at the door to the ground floor, with the noise of the bar behind it. I was desperately trying to find the handle and wrench it open, when it swung away from me, and someone, someone I knew very well, shouted my name above the noise.

'Laureth!'

Mr Woodell can say what he likes, but of all the weird *things* that had happened, this was the weirdest thing of all.

Dad.

Dad was there. I felt his arms go around me, and I knew everything was okay.

## Boy Meets Girl

Also, it's a weird thing about hope. Why is it that when you need it the most, it seems furthest away? I'd given up on ever seeing Dad again, and then he walked right into my arms, and me into his.

Love is a funny thing too. I think I may have already said that, but I'm happy to say it again.

Why is it that sometimes you forget just how much you love someone until they're gone? Why are we so stupid? Shouldn't we always remember that the people we love are more important to us than anything else?

Dad threw his arms around me and burst into tears. So of course I did too. Then he started laughing, so I did that as well, *of course*, and then I shouted so loud in Dad's ear that I think I deafened him.

'Benjamin!' I screamed. 'Benjamin's up there.'

'It's okay,' said Dad. 'It's okay.'

'No! There's a man on the stairs who was trying to—'

'Laureth!' said Dad. 'It's okay. Benjamin's safe. He's over there, talking to a very nice policeman.'

'But he—'

'He just came out of a set of service doors at the side of the hotel. He walked straight up to me and said, "Hello Daddy, we've been looking for you." Cool as you like.'

I laughed again and then started crying some more, and then some other men pushed past us.

'That's the police,' Dad said. 'They'll take care of our friend on the stairs.'

'You know about him?' I said. 'You knew about us?'

Dad laughed.

'Come on,' he said. 'Let's find Benjamin before he wrecks something, and I'll tell you all about it. I got mugged, Laureth! Can you believe that!'

He sounded more surprised than upset about it, just like Benjamin sounds sometimes.

'Mugged?' I asked.

'Uh-huh,' said Dad, and I would have told him off, because this is where Benjamin gets it from. But there were bigger things to think about.

'But what about the cult?' I asked.

'Cult?' said Dad. He sounded confused. 'Listen, let's get Benjamin first. Then we can talk.'

We found Benjamin and Dad managed to get the police to agree that we needed to sleep, and that we'd come along to the police station in the morning to give a statement.

The hotel moved us into 355, because of all the broken glass in 354, but not until Benjamin had been reunited with Stan.

'You could have used something else,' Dad said to Benjamin.

'Sorry, Dad,' said Benjamin.

'What?' I asked. 'To break the lights, you mean?'

'Uh-huh,' said Benjamin.

'He used my laptop,' said Dad. He didn't say it like he was that mad.

'It was the only thing I could see,' Benjamin said, sounding defensive. 'I had to throw it at the lights in the corridor to break them.'

I laughed.

'You did? Is it . . . ?'

'Let's just say,' said Dad, 'that the Benjamin Effect has never been more . . . effective. Just as well I didn't have a new novel stored on that thing, eh? Luckily for me, my daughter had already secured my valuables.'

'That envelope?' I asked. 'Dad, what's going on? Who were those men? Why did they think you had a fortune in your safe?'

'Is that what they thought?

He was silent for a bit, and I knew he was thinking hard.

'Oh,' he said. 'I get it now.'

ᴍᴜᴄ

And then he explained everything, or everything he knew about, anyway. Some of it we pieced together the following day, when we went to the police station. They were interested in two men, prisoners on the run, one of whom had been found tied by his belt to some school gates in Queens, and the other who'd fallen down a stairwell in a hotel in Manhattan, which he and his friend had been snooping around all day.

Dad told us how he'd gone up to Providence, the day before. He'd been getting really desperate about *that* book. He needed to write it, but it just wasn't happening. Thinking he might find something useful, he'd left Switzerland to come to New York to meet the woman at the Poe Museum because he was still fascinated by the Richard Parker story. I guess he didn't tell Mum he was coming, because of the cost of the flight and so on, but he felt it was his last-ditch attempt to make that book work, and then they could stop worrying about money.

On a whim, he'd taken the train to Providence because Poe has some connections there too, and because he wanted to visit the grave of another of his favourite writers who's buried there.

He'd been having a chat on the phone to his editor as he stepped off the train, and just outside the station, he'd been mugged, by the Smoke and the other man.

They'd taken his stuff, all his stuff, and run off.

They'd taken a train straight back down to New

York, because they thought there was a stash of jewellery in Dad's safe. They'd stolen Dad's room card so they knew which hotel he was in, but not the exact room. They'd spent all day watching the rooms from the deli across the street, and had already been thrown out by Margery Lundberg for hanging around the hotel. A maid had seen the Smoke trying Dad's key card in every door on the second floor.

Dad, meanwhile, had been stuck in Providence. He had a thumping headache because the Smoke had whacked him with something.

He had no money, no phone, no passport or ID of any kind, and he told us how in moments you go from being a citizen of the world to a tramp, invisible. He knows a few people in the States, but he couldn't phone anyone.

He realised later he should have gone to the police station straight away but he'd got concussion or something and wasn't thinking straight. He got it into his head he had to go to the British Embassy, and the nearest one was in Boston.

'Boston's fifty miles away,' said Dad. 'In the end I managed to hitch a lift with some old guy driving a truck, which was great, except he turned out to be the only person on the planet without a mobile. So I got to Boston, and you know what I found? It was a public holiday or something and our embassy was shut. So I couldn't get a new passport, and without it, all the banks I tried weren't prepared to give me any money. I was stuck. I tried to find an internet café to email Mum, but you had to pay in all the ones I found.'

Finally, Dad said, he gave up for the night and slept on a bench in the railway station.

Then, that morning, he'd tried again.

Eventually, he wandered into a public library, and it was a librarian who'd saved the day, because she recognised his name.

'You wrote those great books!' she said. 'I love them! Well, the funny ones, anyway.'

Dad was laughing himself silly as he told us that, and the librarian not only loaned him her computer, but a hundred dollars too, of her own money, when he explained what had happened.

He emailed Mum, who picked up the email on her Blackberry at the services on the M6.

She'd gone straight home to organise sending some money to Dad, and then she'd seen a letter sitting on the tray of the printer. Apparently I'd hit the key more than once when I was printing that letter, the letter from Mum and Dad giving me permission to travel on my own, to New York. There were five copies of it sitting there.

Then she'd phoned me. And the police. Who'd phoned the New York Police Department.

And the NYPD had arrived just the same time as Dad got back to the Black King, just as Benjamin walked calmly into the street and up to Dad, and said, 'Hello.'

'Then I told Dad and the police about the bad men,' said Benjamin. 'And they came to find you.'

'But there's still so much I don't understand,' I said.

'Me too,' said Dad. 'But you go first.'

'Well, why did they think you had jewellery in your safe? When all you have is an empty envelope?'

'I've been wondering that too,' said Dad. 'But I think I get it now. Sophie and I were talking about the American contract I've got now, and some rights issues, and then . . .'

He stopped.

'What?'

'I told Sophie I had a great new book idea. It happened on the flight over to New York. You know how I often get ideas when I'm up in the air.'

'So?'

'So you know how she and I always talk about my ideas? If they're any good or not?'

'Oh, Dad,' I said. 'What did you say?'

He chuckled.

'"Diamonds and pearls. And gold. A fortune. Worth millions."'

'The men who mugged you must have overheard and thought you meant it. That you really meant it.'

'I did mean it!' he said. 'I've had the best idea for a book *ever*. And it's worth a fortune. It's in that envelope. That's why I put it in the safe. I wrote it down in my notebook so I wouldn't forget it, but I put it on that piece of paper too, in case I lost the book.'

'Which you did.'

'Ha!' said Dad. 'Yes, I did, didn't I? So I was right to put the idea in the safe.'

He sounded very pleased with himself. He's just like a big kid sometimes.

'What exactly is this amazing idea, anyway?'

'Top secret,' said Dad.

'Oh Dad!' Benjamin and I wailed together.

'Bedtime. But tell you what, I'll show you tomorrow.'

Mum arrived on the first flight she could get, and by lunchtime on Sunday we were all back together, sitting in the deli across the street from the hotel, eating large and complicated sandwiches.

The funny thing is, they weren't even cross. Not one bit. I kept waiting for them to be angry with me, but they just didn't seem to be.

We sat and talked about it all, piecing everything together, and then Dad told us something amazing.

'I'm not going to write that book anymore,' he said, and there was a stunned silence round the table. I felt as if the whole deli was watching us, though I know that's ridiculous.

'About coincidence?' I asked.

'Nope,' he said. 'I've decided it's stupid. There is no such thing as coincidence.'

'What?' asked Mum. 'You've spent the last three million years working on it, and now you've decided there's no such thing?'

'Yep. There is no such thing as coincidence. Think about it. All these guys who've studied it. Jung, Pauli, Kammerer, the others. They tied themselves up in knots trying to show that coincidences have some hidden meaning; secret connections that bring the two things together, yes?'

'Yes, and . . . ?'

'And they're deluding themselves. It's apophenia. Take Pauli and his number. 137. It wasn't even 137! It was 136 point something something something. No one's ever worked it out exactly. But he got obsessed with it the same way Jung and Kammerer and Koestler got obsessed with coincidence.'

'Yes,' I said. 'So?'

'So, think about it. There's only two possible explanations. Either something is total chance. Complete fluke. Just utter randomness that brings things together. Or, on the other hand, one thing has caused the other thing to pop up. In which case, it's not coincidence at all, because there *is* a reason why it happened. A reason founded on causality, right?'

'Er, yes, right,' I said. 'Maybe.'

'So all these men said there was no causality behind coincidences, and then spent years trying to find some other explanation. But that *other explanation* was just another *form* of causality. So there! That's it. Coincidence does not exist.'

We were all silent for a while and then Benjamin said, 'If co-inky-dinks don't exist, then why is Michael's school called number 354?'

'What?' said Dad.

So we told Dad all about Michael. About how the book practically fell on his head, from the train window, as the criminals threw away things they thought were worthless. About how Michael's school was Public School number 354.

'Really?' said Dad. 'That's weird . . .'

His voice trailed off into silence.

'A coincidence, you might say?' said Mum.

'Nope, just chance,' said Dad, coming out fighting. 'Just a very freaky chance.'

I still wasn't sure.

'But what about those pages at the back of your book? That stuff about a death cult, about the secret meaning of coincidence. What was all that about?'

'That?' said Dad. 'That was the beginning of my book. The Hound of Heaven.'

'It was weird,' I said.

'It was a nightmare,' Dad said. 'Did you notice anything about it?'

'It was strange. Odd. Not like the way you usually write.'

'It was 354,' Dad said. 'Each word in turn is three letters long, then five, then four. Over and over again. I was going to write the whole book that way.'

'354? The whole book?'

'Uh-huh,' said Dad. 'To make things more fun, each chapter was also going to be exactly 354 words long. Guess what? I gave up. It took me a whole day to write a page and a half. Slowest bit of writing I've ever done in my life.'

Mum laughed.

'So then, Genius,' she said. 'What's this great idea of yours? The one that's worth millions in diamonds and pearls?'

I heard him slide the envelope across the table and he put my hands on it.

'You open it,' he said. 'And Benjamin can read it.'

I did, and held the piece of paper up for Benjamin to see.

'That's it?' he said. He sounded disappointed. 'Three words?'

'Uh-huh,' said Dad.

'What does it say?' I said. 'Tell me.'

'"Boy Meets Girl",' said Benjamin.

'That's it?' wailed Mum. 'That's your great idea?'

Dad laughed.

'I only needed to write that down to remember,' he said. 'The rest is up here.'

'He's tapping the side of his head with his finger,' whispered Benjamin to me.

'That can have two meanings,' I said, and Dad pretended to be hurt.

'Hey!' he said. 'I'll have you know this is the finest idea I've ever had! I've been thinking. About how Mum and I met. Remember, Jane? It was quite a crazy story, wasn't it? So I'm going to write a book.'

'You are?' said Mum. She sounded amazed.

'Yes,' said Dad. 'I'm going to write a book. A funny one.'

ഗരു

We spent two more days in the city before we came home. Dad told Mum not to worry about the expense. Not since he'd come up with his great idea. When she'd arrived Mum had been pretty cross about the suite Dad was staying in, and told him we couldn't afford it, but Dad said that he was only paying for the cost of a normal room; that they'd given him a free upgrade.

'But it's room 354,' she said.

'So?' said Dad.

'You expect me to believe they upgraded you to room 354?'

There was a long silence then. It was a bit tense. In the middle of the silence, Benjamin suddenly said, 'Oh yeah! That's weird' and I told him to be quiet.

'Yes,' said Dad gently to Mum, 'I do expect you to believe me, Jane.'

And then there was another pause, and then Mum said quietly, 'Of course I do, darling. Of course I do.'

I heard Dad kiss Mum, who giggled like she was young, and Dad told her not to worry about money anymore.

'Diamonds and pearls,' he kept saying. 'Gold dust and fairies' wings.'

∾∾∾

Despite what Dad said, we couldn't stay in New York for long, but there were a couple of things we had to do.

On Monday, we took Mum and Dad to meet Mr Michael Walker. Dad and Michael got on really well, and I felt happy, and later on, we took Benjamin to the comic shop he'd seen and Dad bought him a stack of old comics. While we were in the shop, I thought about Sam, on the plane, and wished for a second I'd taken his number, but only for a second.

Mum was holding my hand as we waited for Benjamin to choose what he wanted. She was describing things in the shop for me, but I suppose my mind was elsewhere.

'You okay?' she said.

'Uh-huh,' I said. 'Yes, Mum. Just thinking about the future.'

'The future? Your future?'

'Yes,' I said.

'Have faith, Laureth,' Mum said. 'Have faith in yourself.'

'Faith? Have faith in myself?'

There was something to think about.

'Yes, why not? We do. I know I get cross with you sometimes, but it's only because I worry about you. But you know, I've decided to stop worrying about you so much.'

*You have?* I thought.

'Trust me,' she said. 'You're going to be a little star.'

'How do you know?' I asked.

'Because you already are, love. You already are.'

That was something else to think about. I smiled to myself, and for once I didn't worry about the smiling thing.

ᶆᶇᶁ

We wandered on through the store and Mum told me about the weird items they had on display, and the titles of some of the more ridiculous comics, and we started giggling.

Benjamin grabbed me.

'Laureth!'

He was so excited he was practically hyperventilating. 'Dad's going to get me all of these. There's *Green Lantern*, and this really old copy of *Batman*, and *The Invisible Man*. He's so cool!'

'That's great,' I said.

'Wouldn't that be amazing? To be invisible? Wow!'

Dad dragged him away to pay for the comics and

I thought to myself; invisible? No, no one should want to be invisible. To have no one notice you, or speak to you. That would be really lonely, in the end.

ᓄᓇ�

The weirdest thing before we flew home was that we had to give a few interviews to some journalists. We'd made the news on both sides of the Atlantic, apparently. People wanted to know why I'd done it, and how, and I told them some of the truth, but not all of it. Maybe I'm learning something from Dad, after all. It was fun, in a way, and though I'm glad we were soon forgotten about, for a while there I felt more visible than I had been in my whole life.

ᓄᓇᕤ

From time to time, Mum would squeeze my hand, and whisper 'thank you' in my ear, and I didn't understand why at first, but as time went by, it began to dawn on me. I think I'd scared Mum and Dad so much that they'd remembered something, something important, something about who we all are, and what matters the most.

They'd both changed.

I could hear it in the things they did, and the way they were with each other, and the way they called each other 'honey'.

ᴍᴖᴕ

But if Dad was done with coincidence, I wasn't.

Maybe he's right, that coincidences don't exist; that they only seem to, that often perhaps we find something amazing only because we forget what a small world this actually is, and how interconnected we are with one another, and with everything in that small world of ours.

But it didn't seem that way to me. I kept thinking about it, about all the crazy links that had to have connected up for this whole thing to have happened, and it freaked me out.

It freaked me out so much, because even if it was just chance as Dad said, and nothing more, the odds of it happening were astronomically tiny.

Maybe something like that will happen to you, one day. Some people would say that the chances are that it will. Think of all those coincidences that almost happened, but didn't quite; all those near misses. Think about all the weird coincidences that must actually have happened, but no one *knew* about them.

ᒲᒲᒷ

Maybe something will happen to you.

Something so weird it makes you stop and think.

As weird as if you picked up a book, maybe even the book you're holding now, looked at the first word of every chapter, and you put them all together, and found a hidden message. Something to make you think, *yes*.

*Yes, that's what we* all *need*.

## *Author Note*

mɔ-ɹ+

One weird idea: to combine two obsessions:
coincidence; and the number 354, and turn them
into a book. It seemed to me that everyone loves
coincidences, feels a shiver of pleasure when they
happen, and yet they're hard to talk about, even
harder to study. Arthur Koestler wrote a famous book
on the subject; but *The Roots of Coincidence* strays
a bit too far into the New Age for me. Carl Jung is
responsible for the most serious study of the subject;
his book *Synchronicity* renamed this curious concept
in an attempt to establish the idea of the meaningful
coincidence. This led him to try to apply statistical
analysis to Astrology, with disputed results, but the
book remains a classic work.

It's almost impossible to make someone else feel something of the excitement you experience from even the most extraordinary coincidence, and, for that matter, the most extraordinary coincidences seem too crazy to be true, they seem, in short, to be fictional. I certainly found that to be the case when something utterly unlikely happened to me – no one I told about it believed it had happened. So I wrote a book about it instead, and *She Is Not Invisible* is the result.

I'd like to take the chance to thank a few people; especially the staff and students of New College Worcester; which is a genuinely inspiring place to visit. I feel very lucky to have spent some time there, and want to thank  Cathy Wright for her endless help; a more professional, friendly and expert librarian you could not hope to meet. I spoke to many students there on my visits, all of them welcoming and delightful company, and I want to thank Beth, Elin, Henry, Jasmine, Jenny and Richard in particular – excellent people one and all. Thanks also to Ellie Wallwork and her father, Simon, for the time they spent with me. Finally, thanks as always to Orion and especially to my editor and publisher, Fiona Kennedy.

And as for my obsession with 354, it seemed only right to work the number into the book in as many ways as possible . . .

Marcus Sedgwick
The black shed
One sunny morn
May Sixth 2013

*She is Not Invisible*

# Reading Group Notes

# In Brief

Sixteen year old Laureth has 'abducted' her little brother, Benjamin. Not abducted in the classic sense, but rather borrowed him to help her take a plane to New York to find their father Jack, a writer, who she believes has gone missing. Her mother doesn't appear bothered that he hasn't been heard from in days, but Laureth's been receiving emails from the mysterious 'Mr Walker' who claims to have found her dad's beloved notebook, the Black Book. Any other sixteen-year-old might attempt to go off and find him on her own, but she needs Benjamin's help – because she's blind.

Benjamin has an uncanny ability, the Benjamin Effect, to crash any electronic device he touches instantly. This causes problems on the plane, when he affects the in-flight entertainment, but proves a godsend at the airport in New York when the failure of the security systems allows them to get through border control despite awkward questions about their status.

Laureth has arranged to meet Mr Walker at the main library in Queens. Her hopes that she'll uncover more about her father's whereabouts from him are dashed when he turns out to be a twelve-year-old boy called Michael, who is far more interested in getting his reward money than in helping Laureth and Ben find their father. Although he does give them a vital clue – a receipt from the Black King Hotel dated just a few days previously.

Despite this sliver of hope, the apparent randomness of Michael's coming across her dad's notebook only adds to Laureth's increasing sense of unease, which is she is keen to keep from Benjamin. When she discovers that Jack has indeed booked into the hotel, but didn't sleep there the night before, her anxiety multiplies, exacerbated by her growing awareness that she's been very foolish taking her brother away without telling her mother anything.

Aware of their father's obsession with his current work in progress, as well as the number 354, Laureth scours the notebook for clues as to where he might be. She learns more about his fascination with coincidence, and the writers and scientists who shared his interest, but nothing that helps her in her quest.

Then Benjamin sees a note at the end of the Black Book, detailing an appointment their father has made to meet someone at Edgar Allan Poe's cottage. That afternoon. The children race across town in pursuit, but again their hopes come to nothing – Jack didn't appear for the appointment.

After an abortive attempt to find their father using 354 as a possible code for an address, Laureth and Benjamin head back to the hotel. There, Laureth receives an email from Michael urging her to meet him back at the railway tracks where he'd found the Black Book. By now really scared by what she's read in Jack's notebook about a death cult, Laureth hurries to the meeting point with Benjamin, discovering on the way that people are looking for them all over New York.

As Michael is explaining how he thinks Jack's notebook might have been thrown from a passing train, they are held up at knifepoint. Michael runs off and the man Laureth refers to as the Smoke, given that he stinks of stale cigarettes, threatens them, demanding the number to the safe in their father's hotel room. The children plead with him that they don't know the code, during which time Michael returns with his brother and some friends, releasing Benjamin and Laureth unharmed.

They learn that Jack was overheard on a train talking about the riches in his hotel safe by the Smoke and his partner, who the children now recognise (by sight and smell) as having been in the deli opposite their hotel earlier that evening. In an attempt to get the loot for themselves the criminals have stolen Jack's wallet, phone and hotel room key and abandoned him in Providence. But since then they have been unable to discover which room he was staying in, hence them following Laureth and Benjamin.

Feeling a little safer now that the Smoke is out of action, they take another taxi back to the hotel and manage to unlock the safe, just as Benjamin spots the Smoke's accomplice crossing the street toward their hotel. Laureth realises he's coming for them and encourages Benjamin to break all the lightbulbs in the room and corridor before escaping, leaving her to grab everything from the safe before getting away herself as her predator stumbles about in the darkened hotel.

She's ecstatic to discover her father in the hotel lobby as she races there, and is soon reunited with Benjamin. Their mother quickly joins them in New York, having discovered what Laureth has done after receiving an email from the abandoned Jack, and finding evidence of the flight to New York at home.

With the family reunited and happy once more, Jack explains that the riches he was overheard talking about was the idea for his new novel, which he'd written down and left in the hotel safe. He also declares, to everyone's amazement, that he doesn't believe in coincidence anymore. Everything, he says, is down to chance.

Laureth looks back at everything that's happened to her over the last few days, and she's really not too sure about that at all.

# For discussion

* What's the book's message, the one you
  can read if you take Laureth's advice
  at the end of the book and link the first
  word in each chapter?

* Discuss the significance of the number
  354. How many times did you spot it?

* Laureth and her father discussed things
  like numinosity and Carl Jung during
  the school run, but her mother preferred
  to talk about food, TV and school.
  What does this tell you about their lives
  and their relationships with Laureth?
  Are things quite as black and white as
  Laureth thinks?

* When were Laureth and Benjamin in the most danger?

* Is she invisible?

* Dad says that coincidences in fiction don't work. Do you agree? Can you think of any novels you've read in which coincidence is an important factor? Did the coincidences work?

* At what point did you realise that Laureth is blind, and how important is it to the story?

* Is Dad right when he says that people aren't interested in other people's coincidences, only their own? What's the greatest coincidence you've ever encountered?

* Laureth is very aware of smells. Do you have any favourite smells that remind you of people you love?

＊ When you were reading the book, did you feel the author was trying to get you, the reader, to spot/predict coincidences that weren't there? Or were they?

＊ The Black Book is white. Michael is black. Laureth doesn't understand colour at all. Is this important?

＊ Laureth says that her mind jumps all over the place but her dad thinks in straight lines. How does this manifest itself in the novel?

＊ What do you think of Sam's reaction to Laureth on the plane?

＊ Laureth. Stan. Jack Peak. Mr Walker. Discuss the importance of these and other names in the novel.

＊ Had you come across the work of Einstein, Pauli, Kammerer, Koestler or Jung before reading this book? Did you know about Richard Parker? If you had, did you learn anything new about them? If not, do you want to learn more?

* Have you ever taken a journey like Laureth's, into the unknown?

* What did you think had happened to Jack?

* Throughout the early part of the novel Laureth is very keen that nobody knows she's blind. Why is this, and what difference does it make to the way you view her as a character?

* Discuss the Benjamin Effect.

* Everyone says they love Jack Peak's books. Well, the funny ones. What do you think of Jack's decision to start writing different kinds of books? Do you think he should write to please himself or his fans?

* Do you think it's just coincidence that Benjamin carries a *Watchmen* rucksack, or is there a comic book superheroes/villains theme running through the novel?

* iPads, iPhones, laptops … How important is technology in *She Is Not Invisible*? How does it make everyone's life easier? And how does it make it harder?

* What do you think about Michael?

* Laureth says that in films and comics there are only two kinds of blind people: pathetic helpless victims of woe and superheroes. Is she correct? Has this book changed the way you feel about blindness?

* Poe's cottage is at 2640 Grand Concourse. 2+6+4+0 = 12. Jack's magic number

is 354. 3+5+4 = 12. Edgar Allan Poe's
most famous poem is The Raven. Ben's
favourite toy is Stan, a raven. Are these
coincidences?

* Who's right – the people who believe in
coincidence or the ones who don't?

* When she goes down the stairs at the
Black King Hotel, Laureth says, 'You
have to pretend you're not scared, even
when you are'. How does she live up to
this statement?

* Discuss the importance of family in *She
Is Not Invisible*.

# Suggestions for further reading

**Novels with lots of coincidences in them:**
Charles Dickens – *Great Expectations*
Thomas Hardy – *Tess of the D'Urbervilles*
Barbara Trapido – *Juggling*
JW Ironmonger – *The Coincidence Authority*

**Poems mentioned in She Is Not Invisible:**
Edgar Allan Poe – *The Raven*
Francis Thompson – *The Hound of Heaven*

**Non-fiction written by people mentioned in this novel:**
Carl Jung – *Synchronicity: An Acausal Connecting Principle*
Arthur Koestler – *The Roots of Coincidence*

# WHITE CROW

'Supposing you wanted to prove something, something important. Supposing you wanted to prove, for argument's sake, that there is life after death.'

'1798, 10mo, 6d. I believe he intends to practice some unholy rite, a summoning, a conjuration. A thing of magic.'wTwo lives, two centuries apart. But they walked the same paths, lived in the same house, became obsessed by the same question.

When city girl Rebecca steps into the quiet streets of Winterfold that relentlessly hot summer her uneasy friendship with strange, elfin Ferelith sets in motion a shocking chain of events.

'an original and exceptional novel'

*The Bookseller*

# MIDWINTERBLOOD

*'I will live seven times and I will look for you and love you in each life. Will you follow?'*

In 2073 on the remote and secretive island of Blessed, where rumour has it that no one ages and no children are born, a ritual sacrifice takes place.

It echoes a moment ten centuries before, when, in the dark of the moon, a king was slain, tragically torn from his queen. Their souls search to be reunited, and as mother and son, artist and child, forbidden lovers, victims of a vampire they come close to finding what they've lost. But can love last forever?

'Marcus Sedgwick is a true original; he writes with a spare, direct simplicity all his own.'

*Independent*